*"I will ne[ver]
but I will make love to
you as no man ever has
before...."*

Kelda had always clashed with her
stepbrother Angelo, and now he was
interfering in her life again, ostensibly on
their parents' behalf. But they both knew
there was more to it than that—there was
unfinished business from that night five
years ago, when Kelda's world had been
turned upside down. Now Angelo was
threatening to make her his mistress. Would
Kelda be able to resist him, or would his
lethal attraction break her heart?

LYNNE GRAHAM was born in Northern Ireland and has been a keen Mills & Boon reader since her teens. She is very happily married to an understanding husband, who has learned to cook since she started to write! Her three children, two of whom are adopted, keep her on her toes. She has a very large wolfhound, who knocks over everything with her tail, and an even more adored mongrel, who rules everybody. When time allows, Lynne is a keen gardener and loves experimenting with Italian cookery.

Books by Lynne Graham

Don't miss any of our special offers. Write to us at the following address for information on our newest releases.

Harlequin Reader Service
U.S.: 3010 Walden Ave., P.O. Box 1325, Buffalo, NY 14269
Canadian: P.O. Box 609, Fort Erie, Ont. L2A 5X3

LYNNE GRAHAM

ANGEL OF DARKNESS

Harlequin Books

TORONTO • NEW YORK • LONDON
AMSTERDAM • PARIS • SYDNEY • HAMBURG
STOCKHOLM • ATHENS • TOKYO • MILAN
MADRID • WARSAW • BUDAPEST • AUCKLAND

ISBN 0-373-11712-4

ANGEL OF DARKNESS

Copyright © 1994 by Lynne Graham.

CHAPTER ONE

'I KNOW this is a shock for you,' Daisy Wyatt murmured uncomfortably, absorbing her daughter's stunned pallor. 'I would have told you ages ago but I was afraid you might be upset.'

'*Might be?*' Kelda raked her rippling Titian red hair back from her brow, a fiery mix of disbelief and temper leaping through her taut frame. 'For goodness' sake, you've been divorced from the man for over four years! Why on earth did you start seeing him again?'

Daisy looked uneasy. Small and blonde and barely into her forties, she was a very pretty woman but right now her face was strained. 'When I heard that Tomaso had had a heart attack, I...I—well...' She stumbled under fire from an outraged emerald-green stare of enquiry. 'I thought it was only decent to write with my good wishes for his recovery and Tomaso wrote me such a kind letter back asking me to visit...I didn't see how I could refuse——'

'But that was three months ago,' Kelda condemned in a shaken tone. 'You've been seeing him all this time and you *never* even dropped a hint!'

Daisy turned a guilty pink. 'At the start, it didn't seem worth mentioning. Just a few friendly visits to the hospital. Tomaso seemed so lonely. He didn't seem to have many visitors, apart...' She hesitated, assessing her daughter's vibrating tension and hurriedly averting her gaze before reluctantly continuing, 'Apart from Angelo, of course.'

That name struck Kelda like a stinging slap on the face. The fact that her sensitive mother wouldn't meet her eyes when she said it didn't help. Indeed, Daisy's visible embarrassment on Kelda's behalf merely piled on the agony. A moment out of time when she was eighteen. Inexplicable... inexcusable. Kelda blocked out the memories threatening her, refusing to recall that dreadful night and its appalling repercussions.

'And I suppose Angelo was as chillingly contemptuous as he was when Tomaso married you and polluted the Rossetti family with a lowly hairdresser!' Kelda snapped with ferocious bite. 'I wish I could believe you cut him dead but I bet you didn't!'

Daisy was studying her tightly linked hands. 'Tomaso and I should never have got married in such a hurry the first time. Angelo hadn't even met me... naturally, he was shocked.'

'Look, I'll make us a cup of tea.' Kelda was so furious, she had to get out of the room before she burst a blood-vessel and said what she really thought. How could her mother make excuses for Angelo? How could she *possibly* do that? When Tomaso Rossetti had married Daisy eleven years ago, his son Angelo had scorned her, snubbed her and treated her as though she was a scheming, common little gold-digger with a greedy eye to the main chance. Kelda's gentle, quiet mother had suffered agonies of discomfiture at Angelo's merciless hands!

Safe in her pine galley kitchen, Kelda snatched in air in heated gasps. Her memories of Daisy's short-lived second marriage were extremely painful. The discovery that Tomaso, for all his apparent devotion to her mother, was having an affair with another woman had shattered Kelda. The divorce had come as an incredible relief. It had freed her from the burden of a secret she had not dared to share with her vulnerable mother, and how could she tell Daisy the truth now? It wasn't even as if she had any concrete proof to offer... nothing more than the dismayed and embarrassed confirmation of a classmate.

There had been a piece about Tomaso in a newspaper. 'Looks as if butter wouldn't melt in his mouth, doesn't he?' Helena had giggled. 'He's had a mistress on the go for years, some blonde he takes to hideaway country pubs for dirty weekends. And even though he only got married recently, he's still seeing her...my father saw them all cosied up together in a dark corner only last week! Holding hands and kissing. Everybody's dying to meet his new wife and see what she's like——'

'She's my mother,' Kelda had said flatly.

Helena had looked aghast. 'Oh lord, I am sorry. I had no idea.'

Hell, why hadn't she told Daisy straight after the divorce? Well quite naturally she had believed the divorce was final. Most divorces were. 'We just weren't compatible,' Daisy had said sadly then, seemingly having no suspicion of Tomaso's infidelity. And now Tomaso had actually had the neck to pop the question a second time! How the heck could Kelda have foreseen that eventuality? And heaven knew, right at this minute, it was a problem she could have done without. She had quite enough problems of her own!

Determinedly, however, Kelda suppressed the bitter awareness that, thanks to all the bad publicity she had received of late, her career as a top model was over. There was no point in crying over spilt milk, she told herself and her poor mother's predicament was far more important.

Kelda had adored her own father, although her recollection of him was unhappily vague, built up on blurred impressions of a jovial, boisterous man, quick to temper, equally quick to laughter. She had only been five when her father began to spend long periods working abroad. She had only a couple of faded photographs of him when he was young and her mother had invariably resorted to tears whenever she tried to talk about him. But she still had every letter her father had ever written to her. The heart attack which had claimed his life in her twelfth year had seemed to devastate her mother at the time...

Yet four short months later Daisy had upped and married Tomaso Rossetti.

Her mother had been the manageress of a small hair salon, Tomaso, an extremely wealthy director in the Rossetti Industrial Bank. According to Daisy, she had been cutting Tomaso's hair for years but she had never once mentioned him to Kelda! Indeed, Kelda had not even had a chance to meet Tomaso before the wedding took place.

The first news she had had of the marriage had been in the headmistress's office at school. Called from class without any prior warning of what was coming, Kelda had been absolutely shattered when she was faced with a strange man with a proprietorial hand at her beaming mother's waist and told he was her stepfather. And she hadn't reacted exactly politely either. She had been appalled, resentful and alienated by the startling fact that the mother she loved could have kept so much from her. It had not been a promising start.

At the time, Kelda and her brother, Tim had been living with an elderly great-aunt in a quiet suburb of Liverpool, seeing their mother on only occasional weekends. Daisy had been unable to find a decent job outside London and her salary had not been enough to run to childcare outside school hours. She had refused to listen to Kelda when she argued that she was old enough to look after herself. Living as she then did in a far from salubrious inner city area, Daisy had been convinced that her children were far better off with their great-aunt.

'We'll all be together now!' Daisy had enthused. 'Tomaso wants us all to be one big happy family. He's bought us a beautiful house in Surrey.'

She could have coped with Tomaso with her hands tied behind her back. It had been Angelo she hadn't been able to handle. Angelo Cesare Rossetti. In the City, they called him the Angel of Darkness. It fitted him like a black velvet glove. Like an avenging dark angel, he destroyed anything and anybody foolish enough to get in his way. In comparison, his father was a positive pussycat, a gentleman of the old school, who treated women like creatures of spun-glass fragility in need of cherishing protection.

While Tomaso and Daisy had regularly scarpered abroad on what seemed to be one long impossibly extended honeymoon during the first years of their marriage, no doubt avoiding as best they could the poisonous atmosphere in their English home, Kelda had been left to Angelo's tender mercies. Angelo, the stepbrother from hell, who had loathed her on sight. Mind you, it had been mutual, she conceded grimly. Even now when she saw Angelo's name in a gossip column she still burned with an unholy, burning hatred that threatened to lick out of control.

As she slammed cups out on a tray, intelligence told her that she should be concentrating on Tomaso's sins, not those of his son. Tomaso, who had probably ordered all his business acquaintances to stay away from the hospital while he plucked violin strings and talked about the misery of his lonely life at the top. Daisy was an easy mark for a sob-story.

Well, never let it be said that Kelda didn't see her duty before her, even when it was unpleasant. The Rossettis had given her poor mother a very rough ride the first time around. Kelda intended to make sure that her mother thought twice, thrice and even more before she took the risk of marrying Tomaso again.

'So when did Tomaso pop the question?' she prompted with a brittle smile as she poured the tea.

'Last night over dinner.'

'He's out of hospital, then.' Kelda had had vague hopes that Tomaso had proposed from his sickbed. Her mother's dreamy expression might then have been excused as compassion.

'For ages. It wasn't a bad attack, more of a warning really,' Daisy shared. 'And Angelo has persuaded him to retire. He knows just how to talk to his father and he's been so kind——'

'Angelo? Kind?' Kelda echoed incredulously.

Her mother tensed. 'He sent a car to pick me up and take me home again every time I visited the hospital.'

'How many near-fatal collisions did it have?'

'Angelo really has been wonderful, Kelda,' Daisy murmured tautly. 'He... he even took me out to lunch. I find him rather overwhelming but he is trying to be friendly and considerate...'

Kelda wanted to laugh like a hyena. Angelo... kind, wonderful, considerate? Only her trusting mother could be so easily taken in. But on another level she was deeply hurt that so much had been happening behind her back. 'Does he know that his father's proposed again?'

Daisy nodded and smiled. Kelda ground her teeth together.

'Angelo even asked about you,' her mother advanced in a clear effort to impress. 'He was very sympathetic and understanding about... well, about that awful business in the papers.'

Kelda went white with rage and mortification and turned her head away. Of course, it had clearly been too much to hope that Angelo hadn't been laughing heartily over her recent sufferings. He never read the tabloids but she just bet that he had made an exception when the gutter Press were tearing her apart. Kelda still felt soiled and besmirched by the lies that had been written about her and the vicious quotes from ex-boyfriends who had jumped on the bandwagon in revenge.

'It's such a shame that you didn't let Danny Philips down more gently.' Daisy sighed regretfully.

'He was a married man!' Kelda reminded her acidly. 'Naturally, I got rid of him as soon as I found *that* out.'

'I expect he didn't mean to fall in love with you,' Daisy murmured sadly.

'He wasn't in love with me... he just wanted to get me into bed like all the rest!' Kelda fielded.

'But he must have been terribly hurt to take an overdose like that, and maybe if you'd gone to see him in hospital——'

'I'd have finished him off!' Kelda broke in rawly. 'He took an overdose because his wife found out he'd been seeing me. He took it to get back in with her and then he spilt his guts in that filthy newspaper to get his own back on me!'

'It was wicked of him to tell all those lies about you.' Daisy's large blue eyes were swimming with tears. 'I told Angelo that you'd never had an affair with anyone...'

'P-Pardon?'

Her mother reddened. 'I wanted Angelo to know that there wasn't a word of truth in any of it. You're not that sort of girl.'

Kelda was in agony. She adored her mother but she had never come closer to killing her! 'Kelda's saving herself for marriage.' She could just hear her mother saying it! And she could see Angelo, struggling not to choke on his wine, sardonically amused by her mother's blind faith in her daughter's virtue. Hellfire embarrassment scorched Kelda.

'Well...what do you think?' Daisy asked hesitantly.

'About what?'

'About me marrying Tomaso again?'

Kelda steeled herself. 'I think you'd be making the biggest mistake of your life. But of course...it's your decision.'

'I suppose the idea of us all being a f-family together is a little fanciful.' Looking stricken, Daisy was visibly swallowing back tears of disappointment.

Kelda felt torn apart by guilt but she reminded herself that it was for her mother's own good. 'Have you given him an answer yet?'

'No,' Daisy conceded tightly.

'If you do marry him, I'll hardly cut you off...I expect we can still meet for lunch occasionally...'

'Y-yes,' Daisy gulped, bending her head. 'But you and I are so close...what about weekends?'

'I will never cross the threshold of any house that harbours Angelo as a regular visitor,' Kelda stated without apology.

'You mean she just dropped it on you?' Her brother Tim burst out laughing. 'Isn't that just Daisy?'

It was the following day. They were lunching in a wine-bar round the corner from the insurance company where Tim worked.

'It wasn't funny! Why didn't you warn me?' Kelda snapped, throwing an icy glance of hauteur at the man at the next table, who had sat fixedly trying to catch her eye ever since she sat down.

Tim followed her gaze ruefully. 'The Iceberg buries another victim...'

'I loathe that stupid nickname!' She set her perfect white teeth into a celery stick and crunched. As she chewed, she flung her head back, her mane of entirely natural pre-Raphaelite curls rippling back over her slim shoulders in tongues of fire. 'Don't use it!'

'OK...OK!' Tim held up both hands in mock surrender.

'Why didn't you tell me she was seeing Tomaso again?'

His mobile features tensed. 'I guessed how you'd react.'

'I bet you said nothing, you lily-livered swine!' Kelda hissed across the table at him. 'You don't care if Tomaso runs around with other women behind her back!'

Tim had gone red. 'I don't think it's any of my business.'

'Oh, I'm all right, Jack!'

Tim grimaced. 'How much of the way you feel has to do with Angelo?'

Kelda froze. 'It's got nothing to do with him!'

Tim gave her an unimpressed glance.

'I can't stand him...that's true.' Her restive hands snapped a carrot stick in two but she held his gaze fiercely. 'But it's Mum's best interests that concern me.'

'You're terrified of Angelo.' Tim looked almost amused.

'Don't be ridiculous...I loathe and despise him...I'm certainly not afraid of him!'

Tim sipped his wine. 'Exactly what did happen the night of your eighteenth birthday bash? You know, I never did find out why Angelo had disappeared, Tomaso looked like thunder and Mum was on the brink of hysterics over breakfast the next morning...'

Every scrap of natural colour had drained from her complexion. 'I don't want to talk about it,' she said tightly.

Her stomach was churning sickly. She broke out in a cold sweat. If she lived to be a hundred, she would still relive that evening in her nightmares. Angelo had humiliated her. Angelo had destroyed her. At a most sensitive age, he had instilled in her an aversion to sexual intimacy that she had still to overcome. The Iceberg was dead from the neck down, she reflected with raw shame and bitterness. She couldn't bear a man to come too close. Her skin crawled when men got seductive and expectant. It made her feel soiled, cheap. Angelo had done that to her...with his scorn and revulsion.

'You're a promiscuous little tramp. It doesn't matter how much money my father spends on you...you will never climb out of the gutter!'

Kelda swallowed back nausea with difficulty. She was lost in the past, savaged by an indictment that had merely heightened the intense vulnerability she concealed from the world.

'Angelo seems to be encouraging Mum and Tomaso,' Tim remarked. 'If I were you, I wouldn't stick a spoke in his wheels.'

'You've seen him, haven't you?' Kelda demanded.

Tim didn't meet her eyes. 'He called into the office one day last week.' He cleared his throat awkwardly. 'Actually, he's offered to fix me up with a better job...'

'I can see I'm on my own,' Kelda breathed flatly.

Tim searched her vibrantly beautiful face anxiously. 'He's a vicious bastard when he's crossed, Kelda. Stay out of it. Mum's a big girl now. Let her make her own mistakes. And if Angelo's prepared to bury the hatchet——'

'I'll lift it out of the ground and bury it in his back,' Kelda slotted in with grim emphasis. 'I have no intention of interfering between Mum and Tomaso but neither have I any intention of being roped in to play happy families. I'm not eighteen any more. I have a life of my own.'

Tim groaned. 'You're not half as tough as you like to act. If you annoy him, Angelo won't just rock your boat, Kelda. He'll blow you out of the water.'

Her hand shook slightly as she raised her glass. Tim's imagery sent a chill snaking down her backbone.

'Any recovery on the career front?' Tim prompted abruptly.

She pulled a face. 'I'm trying to sell my apartment.'

'As bad as that?' Tim looked shaken.

'When the Fantasy campaign dropped me, I lost half my income...and other cancellations followed,' she spelt out tautly.

'But you'll make it up again...you're famous!'

'Notorious,' Kelda corrected with unconcealed bitterness. 'And that's not the sort of image that sells exclusive cosmetics and perfume. My contract with the agency is up in two months' time. I don't think it'll be renewed.'

Tim said something unrepeatable about Danny Philips. Then he smiled. 'You should marry Jeff. He's stood by you and he's got all his Daddy's hotels coming to him——'

Kelda concealed her distaste. She knew she would miss the luxuries her high earnings had brought her but she had no intention of marrying to maintain that lifestyle.

'I should have stopped seeing Jeff weeks ago,' she confided wryly,.

'I liked Jeff.' Tim frowned at her. 'Let him down gently.'

As she dressed for her dinner date that evening, she grimaced. She had already tried and failed twice to let Jeff down lightly. So much for her heartless bitch image! She liked Jeff but he was getting serious. He wasn't the Mr Right her daft mother liked to talk about. Kelda had decided a long time ago that Mr Right didn't exist. Not for her, anyway. She attracted all the wrong types.

The poseurs, the predators. To most men, she was a trophy to show off, a glorified sex object, whose greatest gift was the envious reactions she stirred up among their friends. Five feet nine in her bare feet, Kelda had the sleek slender lines of an elegant thoroughbred and a face that every camera loved. She had flawless skin, gorgeous hair and beautiful eyes. At sixteen she had suddenly blossomed from a gawky, flat-chested late developer into an eye-catching young woman, who turned heads wherever she went. The attention had been balm to a self-esteem continuously battered by Angelo's cruel tongue.

He had so very nearly prevented her from becoming a model. If it hadn't been for the divorce, she would have ended up resitting the final exams she had failed.

'You let her go to London, she'll go wild,' Angelo had forecast. 'She's too immature, too undisciplined and too volatile.'

Angelo had always taken great pleasure in ensuring that whatever she most wanted she didn't get and whatever she least wanted, she got in spades. But she hadn't gone wild, had she? She had clawed her way up the ladder to success and exulted in her first *Vogue* cover. Rather childishly, she recalled reluctantly, she had sent a copy of that edition to Angelo, desperately afraid that he mightn't have seen it. Very childish, she acknowledged. Then, Angelo had always brought out the worst in her character.

Jeff arrived with a massive bunch of red roses and her heart sank. Dinner at a candlelit restaurant followed. No matter how often she tried to tactfully change the subject, Jeff brought it back to marriage. He was like a terrier chasing a bone.

Her conscience smote her. Jeff had staunchly stood by her throughout the tabloid attacks. Other friends had deserted her like rats escaping a sinking ship. Jeff had had touching faith in her innocence. What a shame it was that you couldn't love to order, she thought ruefully. She valued Jeff's friendship but she was beginning to realise that no matter what she did, she was going to lose that as well.

'I'm really very fond of you,' Kelda stressed carefully.

'I don't want you to be bloody fond of me!' he muttered with unexpected heat. 'I want you to marry me.'

'I can't.'

For the remainder of the meal, he swung between arguing and a monolithic attack of the sulks. Kelda managed to charm him out of the worst of his mood but he was drinking too much. Unfortunately she had already agreed to join friends of his at a nightclub. Her attempt to pull out of the arrangement was badly received. Fearful of a public scene, she steeled herself to face what remained of a difficult evening. If it was at all possible, she didn't want to hurt Jeff's feelings.

Belatedly she realised that she had made the wrong decision. In the foyer of the club, Jeff suddenly attempted to drag her into his arms and Kelda slapped his hands away with the fury of a bristling tigress. Of all things, she hated being mauled in public.

'I'm absolutely crazy about you!' Jeff announced stridently. 'Doesn't that mean anything to you?'

'If you don't behave yourself, I'm going home!' she hissed at him in an undertone and turned on her heel, praying that he would cool off.

A split-second later, she stopped dead in her tracks, slaughtered by the sheer shock of finding Angelo less than six feet from her. He had the advantage, she registered. He had seen her first. At six feet four, he was one of the very few men capable of looking down on her even when she was wearing her highest heels.

She was paralysed, her heartbeat quickening, colour flooding her translucent skin and then slowly, painfully draining away again to leave her paper-white. Chillingly dark eyes cut into her like grappling hooks in search of choice and tender flesh. Every tiny muscle in her tensed body jerked tight as she braced herself for attack.

'I presume you do intend to speak, Kelda.' The smooth, cultured drawl sliced through the thickening atmosphere and clawed nasty vibrations of threat down her sensitive spine. He was like a sleek, terrifyingly dangerous black panther about to strike.

'Did you hear someone speak?' she asked Jeff, planting a trembling hand on his arm. 'I didn't.'

She swept past Angelo and his dainty little blonde sidekick with inches to spare and her classic nose as high in the air as she could hold it.

'Do you realise who that was?' Jeff bleated in her ear.

'Once upon a time, my mother was married to his father. That creep was my stepbrother. And we didn't part on such terms that I feel I have to notice him in public.'

'Why didn't you tell me that your mother had been married to Tomaso Rossetti?'

Jeff was so helplessly impressed by anyone whose bank balance was greater than his father's. 'It wasn't important.'

'You just cut Angelo Rossetti dead,' Jeff groaned. 'Are you out of your mind?'

Sitting down, Kelda fought to still the nervous tremors still rippling through her. 'He told me once that I had the manners of a slum child. He ought to be pleased to see how well I've turned out.'

Shock seemed to have sobered Jeff up. 'My father's into the Rossetti Bank to the tune of a million and we're looking for an extension on the loan. I was so shattered by what you did out there, I didn't speak either.' Abruptly, he bolted upright again. 'I'd better go and apologise.'

Her temples were throbbing. 'I'm sorry... I didn't intend to involve you——'

'My God, you must have a death wish!' Jeff muttered. 'Nobody treats Angelo Rossetti like that and gets away with it.'

'I think you'll find that I have,' Kelda asserted with more confidence than she actually felt.

She had gone too far. Temper and other emotions that she had no desire to examine had taken over. Did she never learn? Angelo taunted her and she still went for the bait. The teenage years might be behind her but evidently the responses weren't. Only she could know the depth of the bitter mortification which overwhelmed her in Angelo's radius. Nothing had changed.

Absolutely nothing had changed. In one glance she had learnt that. Angelo had stared her down with freezing hauteur and distaste. The dust beneath his feet would have inspired less repugnance. Of course he hadn't seen her since *that night* ...not once, not even briefly. He had gone abroad and shortly after that their parents had parted. She shuddered under the onslaught of a mess of confused emotions, none of which was pleasant.

Tonight she had reacted in self-defence as she had so often in the past. 'Hit and run' best summed it up, she conceded shamefacedly. If she hadn't got away immediately, her control would have splintered and he would have seen that, caught unprepared, she was vulnerable. Naturally his hostility would be on a high again at the prospect of her re-entering the family circle with her slum-child manners and her legendary promiscuity.

But this time Angelo had been ahead of her. This time he was isolating her. She recognised the subtle brilliance of Angelo's manipulation of her mother and her brother. How come they didn't see it? Frankly, Tim was pleased at the idea of being part of the Rossetti clan again. Tim was always broke, always in debt. Tomaso was open-handed with money.

And Tim, like her mother, had always walked in awe of Angelo. Angelo was so clever that he had finished university in his teens. Angelo spoke half a dozen languages with the sort of fluency that made lesser mortals cringe. Angelo was so dazzlingly successful in the field of international finance that he was currently being tipped to become the youngest ever chief executive of Rossetti Industrial. Tongues that had dared to talk of nepotism had long since been silenced. Everything Angelo touched turned to gold. His opinions were quoted in the serious newspapers. Tomaso thought his son literally walked on water.

'I must say that he was very gracious about it.' Jeff reappeared, exuding an air of strong relief. 'He's asked us to join their table.'

Kelda went rigid. 'But what about your friends?'

Jeff grimaced. 'Don't be so naïve, Kelda. You get an invite like that from Angelo Rossetti and you grab it. He's got influence like you wouldn't believe in all sorts of powerful corners——'

'I'm sorry. I have a dreadful headache.' Kelda stood up, her face a mask of disdain. 'You can call a cab for me if you like——'

Slowly he shook his head. 'Kelda...'

She was immovable. Catch her falling for a trick like that? No way would she give Angelo the opportunity to put her down in front of an audience. He excelled in that direction. Time was when she wouldn't have had the wit to forestall him... time was when she would have waded in with both fists metaphorically flying, unconcerned by the presence of others. Suddenly she was unbelievably grateful to be a mature twenty-four, rather than an insecure, dreadfully unhappy teenager, trying to act older than she was.

Jeff was furious. She was wryly amused at the way the prospect of making an influential contact had cleared his wits and turned him off his previous insistence that he loved her and wanted to marry her. Insisting that he go and find his friends, she went home alone.

Switching on the lights in the lounge, she kicked off her shoes and switched on her answering machine. Nothing. Once there would have been at least a couple of messages. Not now...she was yesterday's news. The Iceberg, who drove innocent married men to suicide. Her apartment would sell for far less than she had paid for it. Her bank balance was at an all-time low. She had had insurance for accident or injury but nothing to cover what amounted to being virtually unemployable. The media had turned her into a figure of hate. There had been plenty of pictures of Danny's tear-stained, plain little wife. The wife that Kelda had not even known existed, living in the country as she did with their two young children while Danny had lived the life of a free and easy single man in the city during the week.

He had actually told Kelda that he went home most weekends to his elderly parents! With a sudden choked sound between a laugh and a sob, Kelda covered her working face with two unsteady hands. How could she have been so stupid? And how could Danny have told so many lies? For the money, she thought cynically. The true story would have made surpassingly unexciting reading. Danny had made her look like a vicious bitch, who used men up like tissues and threw them away when she got bored. And the truth...really the truth was far more pathetic, she reflected.

Here she was all dressed up in the proverbial sexy little black dress which showed off her perfect curves and endless legs and what *was* she, she asked herself painfully as she stared at her reflection in one of the mirrored wardrobes in her bedroom. A complete fraud! Less of a woman certainly than Danny's poor little wife, who loved him and had borne his children and who had apparently been willing to forgive and forget from the instant he landed in that hospital bed!

What did it feel like to love like that? She couldn't imagine it...she had never loved, only once experienced the devastation of desire...and *that* she never ever allowed herself to remember. It had hurt so much and so badly; she had been savaged by her own vulnerability. Deep down inside the pain was still there like an indoor alarm system. A man put his arms around her and if she felt anything at all, the alarm went off. *If he makes me want him...what then?* And she would go cold, inside and out.

The intercom buzzed beside the front door. It was two in the morning. With a crease between her brows, she pressed the button.

'Angelo here...'

Kelda's stomach clenched fearfully. She leapt back a step.

'Go away!' she shouted.

She heard muffled speech as if he had turned to speak to someone else.

'Calm down, *cara*,' Angelo purred.

Her lashes blinking in bemusement at the smooth endearment, Kelda let rip again, something terrifyingly akin to hysteria audible even to herself in her shrieked response. 'Leave me alone!'

She walked away from the front door, breathing fast, and backed into the lounge where she sat down on the sofa and wrapped both arms round herself tightly. She had had a lousy evening, a lousy week, a lousy month come to that. She was not in the mood for a fight with Angelo. Dimly she had known that it would come, but she hadn't been prepared for it to happen so soon.

It was with utter disbelief that she heard her front
door open. She lurched bolt upright in genuine fear,
cursing herself for not using the chain.

'Do you think I should call a doctor, Mr Rossetti?' a
vaguely familiar male voice enquired. It was the night
security guard.

'No...I don't think that will be necessary now that I
am here. Thank you again.'

'It's a pleasure to be of service, Mr Rossetti.'

She heard the crackle of money changing hands and
she still couldn't move or react. She couldn't believe that
Angelo had somehow contrived to break into her very
secure apartment with the assistance of the guard.

Angelo appeared in the doorway.

'If you don't g-get out, I'll call the police!' Kelda
screeched at him.

CHAPTER TWO

KELDA had blocked Angelo out in the foyer of the nightclub. She had seen him and yet she hadn't seen him. Her eyes had skipped off him again double quick, discarding the imagery as if it burned. And it did...it did. Angelo was drop-dead gorgeous.

'My, but you're pretty,' she had trilled the very first time she met him at the age of thirteen, derisively scanning the near-classic perfection of his golden features and the lean, lithe perfectly balanced body that went with it. Amazingly, Tomaso had laughed. Angelo hadn't.

And then as now, Kelda had somehow found herself still staring, after the laughter had died away. He had the slashing cheekbones of a Tartar prince, long-lashed, brilliant dark eyes and a strong aristocratic nose. The whole effect was sexually devastating. She hadn't known what made him so disturbing when she was thirteen...but she did now.

Angelo was sinfully, scorchingly sexy. It hit the unwary like a forcefield of raw energy. The very air seemed to sizzle round Angelo and when you reached a certain age, she acknowledged, that certain age when you often embarrassed yourself with your own thoughts, you would look at a male like Angelo and find yourself quite unable to avoid wondering what he was like in bed...

A little voice inside Kelda's head cruelly reminded her that she was not entirely unaware of what Angelo was like in bed...and instantaneously a wave of mortified heat engulfed her translucent skin. It was hardly surprising that such painful imagery should visit her now. This was the first time they had stood face to face since that ghastly, unforgettable night over six years ago.

23

'The police,' Angelo reminded her with satire. 'Weren't you about to call them? Or have you decided that you really can't afford the publicity?'

As Kelda's teeth gritted, she made a swift recovery from her unfortunate loss of concentration. 'How did you persuade the guard to let you in here?

'I told him you were suicidal,' Angelo drawled softly. 'And you probably will be by the time I'm finished with you.'

'Get out!' Kelda gasped. 'Get out of my apartment!'

'It's not going to be your apartment for much longer.' Angelo cast her a veiled glance of cruel amusement. 'In the current market, I suspect you are about to suffer from a severe negative equity problem... the sale price is not going to wipe out the mortgage debt——'

'Damn, you to hell!' Kelda interrupted tremulously. 'I know what negative equity is. I'm not stupid——'

'You just didn't manage to pass a single exam in all those years of expensive education,' he inserted.

'I'm thick,' Kelda responded through clenched teeth, refusing to rise to the bait.

'Surpassingly so,' Angelo agreed. 'If you had listened to me, you could have had the modelling career *and* the education to fall back on. As it is, you have neither——'

'I can't believe you actually came here just to crow!' Kelda blistered back.

'I want you to understand your present position,' Angelo breathed almost conversationally. 'If you think that your future is on the skids now, you're wrong. Life could become so much more painful... with a little help from me.'

The assurance hung there in the pulsing air between them and her blood ran cold in her veins. She cleared her throat. 'Are you threatening me?'

'Surprised?' Angelo sank down with innate grace into a wing-backed armchair and surveyed her with total cool.

'I have no intention of allowing you to come between my father and your mother a second time...'

Her tongue snaked out to wet her dry lips. 'A second time?'

'You put considerable stress on their relationship six years ago——'

Rigid with incredulity, Kelda spat, 'That's a filthy thing to say!'

'But true, and this time matters were proceeding smoothly until once again you intervened——'

Kelda was shaking. 'I don't know what you're talking about!'

A satiric brow climbed. 'Last night, Daisy asked my father to give her more time to consider his proposal, and we both know why, don't we?'

Kelda thrust up her chin. 'Naturally she wants to think it over very carefully. You can't blame me for that. For goodness' sake, she divorced him five years ago!'

'You selfish little bitch,' Angelo murmured with a softness that was all the more chilling than a rise in volume. 'Daisy didn't have any reservations until *after* she saw you yesterday!'

Kelda stiffened, colour flying into her cheeks. Derisive dark eyes raked over her, absorbing her sudden tension.

'She's afraid of losing her daughter, would you be-lieve?' Angelo drawled. 'Family ties are very important to Daisy. What the hell did you say to her?'

'Nothing that I wouldn't say again!' Kelda slung defiantly, although the ache of tears threatened behind her eyelids. 'And if she is having second thoughts, don't lay them all at my door. Your father wasn't exactly Mr Fidelity the first time around and maybe she suspects that!'

Angelo's striking bone-structure clenched hard. 'I told you that there was absolutely no truth in those alle-gations years ago,' he grated with savage emphasis. 'And if you have repeated those same lies to Daisy, I'll break every bone in your poisonously vindictive little body!'

Shocked by the depth of his anger, Kelda paled and drew back a step, but she was outraged by his treatment. No, she had no concrete proof to offer her mother on the subject of Tomaso's adulterous affair but, the year before their parents had separated, Kelda had flung that allegation at Angelo.

And for a fraction of a second Angelo's expression had one hundred percent convinced her that he knew exactly what she was talking about and that he was well aware of his father's extra-marital relationship with another woman. Kelda had taken him by surprise and his complete denial of that relationship had come just that little bit too late to be plausible.

Angelo had known all right. And no doubt, Angelo hadn't seen anything the slightest bit immoral in Tomaso's behaviour. In his world, married men with mistresses were far from unusual. But that same knowledge would have destroyed her mother. Now, Kelda found herself wondering if indeed her mother had at least suspected Tomaso of having another woman. It was quite possible that Daisy would have kept that information to herself, rather than share it with her teenage daughter.

'What did you tell her?' Angelo demanded ferociously.

'I told her nothing...not that that is any of your business,' Kelda stressed.

'When my father's happiness is at stake, it *is* my business.'

'I doubt if he'd thank you for your interference...and if my mother knew that you were here threatening me like this——'

'Are you planning to tell her?' Angelo had the stillness of a jungle cat about to spring.

Kelda wouldn't have dreamt of telling Daisy, but she was furiously angry and she lifted a bare pale shoulder in a deliberately provocative gesture. 'I might...on the other hand I might not,' she said sweetly, incandescent green eyes flaming at him. 'You'll just have to wait and see, won't you, Angelo?'

He had gone satisfyingly white beneath his bronzed skin, his facial bones harshly set. Kelda smiled, widely, brilliantly, smugly. It really had been very foolish of Angelo to come here and threaten her. Astoundingly foolish... astoundingly out of character for so noted a tactician. One lean brown hand was curled into his fist and without warning he stood up again.

'I came here tonight to appeal to your better nature——'

'I haven't got one, Angelo... not where you're concerned,' she said shakily but truthfully.

'I could break you with one hand,' Angelo savoured, eyes as treacherous as black ice on a wintry night, fixed to her with savage intensity. 'And I will... I don't mind waiting a little while... a very little while. And while I'm waiting, you'll be waiting too...'

Icy fingers were walking up her unbelievably taut backbone. Angelo hated her, he really did hate her. And she knew why. It lay unspoken between them, untouched but raw. She shivered, no longer able to meet that hard, dark scrutiny. Had she gone overboard? Should she for once have kept her mouth shut? But why should she stand and take abuse from Angelo?

Her front door shut with a soft click. Shaking all over now, released from the spell he always cast, Kelda collapsed down into the nearest seat. She felt sick. He had called her poisonous, vindictive, and yet all she wanted was her mother's happiness. Had it been selfish to make it clear that if Daisy married Tomaso again she was unlikely to see so much of her adored daughter?

But hadn't that only been the truth? She couldn't stand Angelo, and the savage hostility between them would be painfully obvious to both their parents. It would hardly add to connubial bliss, so naturally her contact with her mother would have to take place only when Angelo was elsewhere. Was that her fault? Was that so horribly selfish of her? Tears lashed her eyelids in a scorching surge. The memories were coming back...

Yes, she had bitterly resented her mother's remarriage all those years ago. Had she had a chance to get to know Tomaso in advance, had she even known of his existence, maybe she would have reacted differently.

The sudden material change in their lifestyle hadn't helped. Kelda had been parcelled off to an exclusive boarding school where her accent had provoked her classmates to pitying laughter. Her friends, her great-aunt, everything that had given her security had been wrenched away all at once. Instead of seeing more of her mother, she had actually seen less of her. Was it really any wonder that she had found it so hard to adapt?

The worst shock had been the discovery that, when their parents were abroad, Angelo was expected to take responsibility for her. Angelo ruled with an iron rod. When she was expelled from that first school for going 'over the wall' one night on a dare, it had been Angelo who took charge and reinstalled her in a convent day school with more rules and regulations than Holloway. It had been Angelo who took her apart when she failed her exams, Angelo who forced her to spend several fruitless vacations swotting with private tutors as bored and fed up as she was.

Tomaso had seemed to find his son's assumption of authority amusing. When he was around, which had been rarely, he hadn't interfered. Her mother had had a tendency to slip out of the room when Kelda appealed to her for back-up. Defying Angelo to her last gasp, Kelda had refused to work. She had frequently been in trouble at school but she hadn't cared because for the first time in her life she had been really popular.

At sixteen, Angelo had trailed her screeching out of her first boyfriend's car. She had sneaked out on the date, conscious that her mother would think that Josh at twenty-two was too old for her. The evening had been spent at a ten-pin bowling alley...nothing could have been more innocuous. Josh had parked his car a hundred yards before the entrance of the house on the way back. He had been on the brink of giving her a kiss... only on the brink, mind you, when all of a sudden the door was wrenched open and she was forcibly hauled out of Josh's reach by Angelo.

'Approach her again and I'll break every one of your fingers,' he had told Josh with a chilling smile. That had been the end of that, and the word had gone out on her locally. Josh had talked. Date Kelda and you tangled with Angelo Rossetti. Not surprisingly, it had destroyed her social life. Even her girlfriends had laughed and, not content with humiliating her, Angelo had told Tomaso and Daisy, ensuring that what little freedom she had had was even more severely curtailed. He had made Josh sound like a potential rapist.

Was it any wonder that she had hated Angelo? Even now, it still stuck in her throat that she had had to endure all those years of Angelo's moralising lectures. What about his own reputation?

From birth, he had made headlines. When Tomaso and his far richer Brazilian wife had split up, Angelo had been the most fought-over little boy in the Western world. Tomaso had lost, but when his ex-wife died he had fought for custody again, this time against Angelo's grandmother. Tomaso had won the final battle, but he hadn't managed to subdue the explosive temperament that powered his son.

Angelo's teenage exploits had shocked Europe. At the age of eighteen, he had inherited his late mother's millions, and for several years afterwards he had run wild. He had lived the self-indulgent life of the super-rich playboy. His insatiable appetite for beautiful women had been notorious. His sex-life might have become considerably more discreet over the last decade but husbands still paled in Angelo's vicinity.

As her mind threatened to leap forward to her eighteenth birthday, Kelda tensed and stopped her recollections stone dead in their tracks. She went to bed, suppressing all thoughts on the subject of Angelo's threats... after all, what could he possibly do to her?

Dawn was lightening the sky beyond the curtains when she woke up, shivering and perspiring, an hour later. She had been wrestling with the duvet, probably crying out. The fear was still with her even in the light of day. The nightmare had been so real.

Getting up, she poured herself a glass of mineral water in the kitchen. On wobbly legs, she sank down at the breakfast-bar and stared into space. She had been allowed to throw a party to celebrate her eighteenth birthday. Owing to her exams, the party had been held several months after her actual birthday. There had been two events to celebrate. Her birthday and the end of her schooldays. Daisy and Tomaso had gone out for the evening but naturally Angelo had had no such tact. Strange to think that some hours after that wretched party had started she had been desperately, pathetically grateful that Angelo had stayed home.

Before the party had started, Angelo had staggered her by complimenting her on her appearance. Ignoring her dropped jaw and looking oddly self-conscious, he had then taken himself off to his suite of rooms on the far side of the house. He had just come home after a long period working abroad and it must have been almost a year since she had seen him. After that astonishing compliment, she had actually wondered if her stormy relationship with Angelo was miraculously about to improve with his acceptance that she was now an adult.

She had promised that there would be no alcohol at the party but most of her guests had brought wine. Reluctant to be the odd one out, Kelda had had a couple of glasses. Half a dozen boys had shown up on the doorstep midway through the evening. One of them had been the brother of one of her best friends, so she had let them in.

It had happened in the library. Some people had drifted in there and she had had to shoo them frantically out again because the party had been getting rowdy and there were far too many valuable objects in that room. She should have called for Angelo's help then, because she had known that some people had had far too much to drink. But most of those people had been her friends.

She had been switching out a lamp when she was grabbed from behind. Having believed that she was alone in the room, she had screamed with fright. For a moment, she had assumed it was one of the boys she knew fooling around, but when she was dragged down on the carpet by bruising hands and a crude voice started telling her in the kind of language she had never heard before exactly what he was going to do to a 'snobby little cow' like her, she had been terrified out of her wits.

He had been so strong. Until that night she had never properly appreciated just how much stronger the average male was in comparison to a woman. She had gone wild, trying to kick, trying to claw with her nails while he yanked her dress up round her waist and bit horribly at the exposed slope of her breasts. He had hit her a stunning blow across the side of her head and then he had put his hand over her mouth, depriving her of the ability to scream. She'd been involved in a desperate struggle when the light went on and all of a sudden she was freed.

She had thrown up on the priceless Persian rug at Angelo's feet. Her assailant had taken immediate flight. She had not seen his face and, strangely, Angelo had made no attempt to stop him. He had simply swung on his heel and walked back out of the room to tell everyone that the party was over. At that point, she had been too hysterical to realise that Angelo had *not* understood what he had interrupted.

Stumbling and crying, she had fled upstairs to her bedroom. She had stripped and got into the shower, needing to wash away the taint of the hands that had touched her. There had been bruises on her breasts and a lump the size of a small egg on the side of her head where she had been struck. The attack had terrified her and she had been sitting still shaking on the side of her bed when Angelo knocked and entered.

'A promiscuous little tramp', he had called her and, still suffering from the effects of shock, Kelda had looked back at him numbly, unable even to credit that he could think she had been writhing about on the library floor in the dark out of choice.

'He attacked m-me!' she had gasped. 'He was trying to rape me . . .'

And she still remembered the way Angelo had looked at her. He had been so pale, so rigid with tension. She had recognised the seething anger he was struggling to restrain. It had glittered dangerously in his piercing dark eyes like a violent storm warning. For a foolish moment she had actually thought that he believed her and that he was angry with himself, angry that he had allowed her assailant to get away instead of calling the police to report an assault. But his next words had demolished that hope.

'You disgust me,' he had breathed in a savage undertone. 'I will never forget what I saw tonight.'

He had not even given her a fair hearing, had not hesitated in choosing to believe the very worst of her. His response, following so closely upon the attack she had endured had reduced her to stricken sobs. It had been some time before she pulled herself together again, and then the anger and the fear of what he would tell her mother and Tomaso had assailed her.

She hadn't thought about what she did next. Had she known what would happen, she would have stayed where she was, safe in her own room . . . but she had been distressed and frightened and helplessly determined that Angelo should hear her side of the story and believe her. She hadn't stopped even to put her dressing-gown on.

She had knocked on Angelo's door. Although she had been able to see faint light beneath the door, there had been no answer. She had crept in. The bedside lamp had cast a soft pool of light over Angelo. He had been asleep and about that point, her memory became confused between what she did recall and what, for a long time afterwards, she had refused to admit even to herself.

A white sheet had been riding dangerously low on one lean golden hip. He had been naked and she had been strangely hesitant about waking him. Indeed now, when she was of an age when she had learnt to be truthful at least with herself, she could admit that she had been mesmerised by his sheer masculine beauty. For the very first time, she had reacted to Angelo's physical allure. He had not been Tomaso's son, her hatefully arrogant stepbrother, who just so happened to be very good-looking. No, it had been much more personal, much more intimate than that, and the sensations Angelo had aroused in her had been painfully new to her experience.

He had opened his eyes, pools of passionate gold. He had not appeared to be still half asleep. But perhaps he had been. Something had flamed in that golden gaze that raked over her while she had hovered there in stupid paralysis and he had reached up with two very determined hands and pulled her down on to that bed with him.

'*Carissima... bella mia,*' he had breathed passionately against her lips in welcome, suggesting that he had inexplicably mistaken her for someone else. He could not possibly have been addressing those endearments to Kelda.

'Angelo!' she had gasped incredulously before he silenced her with the heat of his mouth.

It had not been to her credit that she had neither screamed nor raised a finger to fight him off. But the terrible truth was that she had had no thought of denying him. In fact she could not recall a single thought of anything passing through her blitzed mind during those fevered few minutes.

The explosion of desire, of need, of want had been instantaneous. The stab of his tongue into the moist interior of her mouth had drowned her in waves of intense physical pleasure. She had been reduced to mindless compliance within seconds. Angelo kissed with electrifying eroticism. She had wrapped her arms round him with shameless abandonment and the spell had only been broken when a thunderous male voice rudely interrupted them.

'You set me up!' Angelo had hissed incomprehensibly, staring down at her with cold, embittered fury.

Even six years after the event, Kelda still got hot and cold reliving that hideous moment when Angelo had released her and she had dazedly focused on Tomaso standing at the foot of the bed. Ignoring her, Tomaso had been ranting at his son in staccato Italian. Normally a mild-mannered man, Angelo's father had been shocked and completely enraged by the scene he had interrupted.

But then, oddly enough, Tomaso had briefly appeared to calm down. He had even managed a rather grim smile as he said something very clipped. Whatever Angelo had said in response had wiped that smile right back off his face again and two seconds later Tomaso had been ripping off his own jacket, draping it round Kelda's cowering shoulders and practically trailing her out of the room while throwing words that had sounded positively violent over his shoulder at his son. His precious, much beloved son...

Daisy had come to her bedroom. Kelda had striven to explain the inexplicable but tears had overwhelmed her. 'Just put it behind you, darling,' her mother had whispered, in sympathetic tears herself. 'I know you must feel very foolish but at your age one does do foolish things...that's a fact of life...and it's so hard to control your feelings but you'll get over him...'

Her mother had assumed that she had thrown herself at Angelo's head because she was infatuated with him, and Kelda had been too deeply ashamed of her behaviour and too desperately confused to protest. She hated Angelo and yet when he had touched her she had gone up in flames. It had not been the sort of self-discovery she could have shared with her mother.

Angelo had read her appearance by the side of his bed as a sexual invitation. Why he should have done so and why he should have acted on such an invitation, she had never understood. Angelo had never given her the remotest hint that he considered her even passably attractive. Could he *really* have mistaken her for another woman? She found that explanation unlikely. So why had he touched her? To humiliate...to hurt...and when had he planned to stop?

The next morning, Angelo had been gone. He had had an apartment in London. Her stepfather had heavily assured her that he attached absolutely no blame to her. She was innocent of all fault, he had stressed, making her feel guiltier than ever. She had felt so dreadful for causing a rift between father and son. When she had fought her embarrassment enough to mumble, 'Angelo didn't mean to——' Tomaso had grimly silenced her with the reminder that Angelo was eight years older.

Her mother had said later, 'I can't reason with Tomaso. He's very strict about some things and even though I assured him that it was only a few kisses, he won't listen to me. He said that he can no longer trust Angelo with you and he's very angry with him. I think he told Angelo to get out and that must have been devastating for both of them. Until now, they were so close...'

Angelo had accused her of setting him up. How, she had no idea, had never wanted to know, because frankly the way things had turned out afterwards she might as well have set him up. His father had told him to leave and she had been relieved of all responsibility for the episode. A couple of days later, she had travelled over to France with a girlfriend and her family for a month's holiday and while she had been away she had received a letter from her mother, telling her that she was separating from Tomaso.

Had that been her fault? She was much inclined to say no. In the months coming up to that fatal night, she had noticed that Daisy was far from her sunny self. There had been something wrong in that relationship then, some tension that had had nothing to do with what had later happened between Angelo and her.

Dear lord, she suddenly reflected, why had her mother had to get involved with Tomaso Rossetti again? And the second she thought that, she despised herself. How could she be so selfish? Had Tim been right to suggest that her hostility towards the idea of Tomaso and Daisy remarrying related more to her own hatred of Angelo than to any genuine concern for her mother's future happiness?

Mid-morning the next day, she received a call from Ella Donaldson, who ran the modelling agency she had been with since she was eighteen. 'I've got a last-minute booking for you... if you're not too proud to take it,' she announced.

Kelda bit at her lower lip, gathering that the assignment was downmarket and less lucrative than what had once been offered to her.

Ella didn't wait for her reply. 'A holiday brochure. A very upmarket company, mind you... St Saviour Villas. Mr St Saviour himself strolled in here not half an hour ago and made a personal request for you, and let me remind you,' Ella said drily, 'right now, personal requests for you are like snow in high summer.'

'I do appreciate that,' Kelda put in tightly. Her interview with Ella Donaldson a month ago had been very unpleasant. A tough, astute businesswoman, Ella didn't give two hoots about whether or not Danny Philips had been lying. Her sole angle had been Kelda's stupidity in

leaving herself open to such damaging publicity. The
agency had lost a big commission when Kelda was
dropped from the Fantasy campaign.

'Good. Mr St Saviour thinks you're a very classy
looking lady...' Ella told her. 'But he did beat me down
on your usual fee——'

'Yes.'

'Someone else must have dropped out last minute,'
Ella asserted. 'Otherwise he wouldn't be wanting you
airborne by tomorrow afternoon——'

Kelda frowned. '*That* soon?'

'You're free until Monday,' Ella reminded her. 'The
shoot is in Italy... you should be home by Saturday.
They're using a photographer I've never heard of but
you can't afford to quibble. The other models are Italian.'

Kelda replaced the phone after Ella had finished ad-
vancing flight details. Italy...tomorrow. She'd have gone
for the cost of the flight, she acknowledged inwardly,
just to get away for a while. The next morning, she tried
to phone her mother but Daisy was out. She called Tim
at work instead and told him where she would be.

It was late when her flight landed at Pisa. Her name was
called out over the public address system and she was
greeted at the desk by a morose little man, who merely
verified her identity and his own before sweeping up her
case and leaving her to follow him out to the taxi.

Their destination was a villa complex in the La Magra
Valley, somewhat off the tourist track as befitted an exclusive development. Kelda had never been to Tuscany
before in the past, she had had assignments in both Rome
and Milan but, tightly scheduled as her timetable had
been then, she had never had the opportunity to ex-
plore. Her expressive mouth tightened ruefully. It was
a little late to wish that she had taken more time off at
the height of her popularity. Now she no longer had the
luxury of choice. She would have to take any work that
came her way just to survive.

It was too dark for her to appreciate the scenery and she rested back her head and dozed, waking up with a start when the door beside her opened and cooler air brushed her face.

Her driver, surely the most unusually silent Italian male she had ever met, already had her case unloaded. Climbing out, Kelda stared up at the dim outline of what looked like a medieval wall towering above them. A huge studded oak door was set into the wall. Kelda frowned. The door looked more like it belonged to a convent than a hotel. Her driver tugged the old-fashioned bell and headed back to his car.

An old woman appeared in the dark doorway.

'Signorina Wyatt,' Kelda introduced herself.

'*Sorda.*' The woman smiled and touched one ear and shrugged. Then she pointed to herself and said, 'Stella.'

Did she mean that she was deaf? Grabbing her case up, Kelda followed her across a vast unlit courtyard. A huge building loomed on three sides. Her companion ushered her into a big tiled hall that looked mercifully more welcoming than what she had so far seen. No reception desk though...and it was so silent.

As she climbed a winding stone stair in the older woman's wake, she smiled to herself. For sheer character, this place beat all the luxury hotels she had ever stayed in! As for the silence, this was not high season and they were off the beaten track. It was also pretty late and the other models were undoubtedly in bed, preparing themselves for the shoot at some ungodly hour of the morning.

Stella showed her into a panelled room of such impressive antiquity and grandeur that Kelda hesitated on the threshold. A giant four-poster bed, festooned with fringed damask hangings, dominated the room. A door in the panelling was spread wide to display a bathroom of reassuringly modern fixtures. French-style windows opened out on to a stone balcony, furnished with a lounger and several urns of blossoming flowers.

The bathroom was hung with fresh fleecy towels, furnished with soap and an array of toiletries such as were the norm in any top-flight hotel. The sight was indefinably reassuring. Kelda found herself looking for the list of rules that every hotel had somewhere and, while she was glancing behind the bathroom door, Stella disappeared.

With a rueful laugh, Kelda frowned at the closed bedroom door through which Stella had wafted herself at supersonic, silent speed, and then her attention fell on the tray of hot coffee and sandwiches sitting on a cabinet beside the bed.

She didn't like to drink coffee last thing at night and she looked for a phone. There wasn't one. She went to the door and then hung back. Maybe it wouldn't be a good idea to go demanding mineral water to drink at this hour if Stella was the only member of staff on duty.

Undressing, she treated herself to a quick shower to freshen up. With a sigh, she allowed herself one sandwich and two sips of coffee before climbing into the gloriously comfortable bed. She thought it funny that nobody from the crew had come to greet her, not even the photographer, keen to issue instructions for the shoot in the morning. Maybe a taste of fame had made her too self-important, she scolded herself. And she certainly couldn't complain about the standard of accommodation allotted to her. Within minutes of switching out the light, she was fast asleep.

'*Buon giorno, signorina . . .*'

'*Buon* whatever,' Kelda mumbled, stretching sleepily and opening her eyes as the curtains were pulled back, flooding the dark room with brilliant sunshine. As she sat up, she registered that the voice had been male and hurriedly hauled the sheet higher, thinking that if someone had to come into her room when she was asleep, she would have infinitely preferred a maid to a waiter.

'*Giorno,*' he sounded out with syllabic thoroughness.

And a blasted irritating waiter come to that, set on educating her, she thought grumpily or maybe what was really irritating her was the fact that the unfortunate man sounded horrendously like Angelo. One of those growlingly sexy accents all Italian males were probably born with. Like a cut-throat razor wrapped up in smooth black velvet, contriving to be both riveting and unnerving simultaneously.

She shaded her eyes to focus on the offender and nearly dropped the sheet. Her emerald-green eyes incandescent with disbelief, she gasped, 'A-Angelo?'

CHAPTER THREE

'WELCOME to my lair in Tuscany.' Angelo uncoiled himself from his inexpressibly relaxed lounging stance against the French windows he had thrown wide and strolled to the foot of the bed.

Thinking she was in some impossibly realistic nightmare, Kelda didn't bother about proudly holding her ground. She jack-knifed back against the carved wooden headboard and simply gaped at the virile vision of masculinity her crazy mind had conjured up out of thin air. He looked good even in a nightmare, but for some reason he was dressed for riding. Long black boots, thigh-hugging breeches of positively indecently faithful fit and a black cotton sweater that lent him a devilish aspect. He wasn't real...he absolutely wasn't real, and if she shut her eyes again he would go away. She did so.

'Clearly you don't quite function at the speed of light when you wake up alone,' Angelo drawled in a tone that sent hideously responsive tremors down her rigid spine. 'I can change that. And from where I'm standing I'm very well satisfied. You look really hot mistress material. I thought you might look a little worn at this hour without the cosmetic tricks of the trade, *cara*...'

Kelda's long lashes swept up like fans. She swallowed hard.

Angelo was leaning in a very familiar way on the footboard, lustrous golden eyes wandering intently over every exposed inch of flesh above the sheet. 'All those lovers...all those different beds,' he extended. 'I was expecting to be just a tiny bit disappointed...but I'm not. You look all dewy and untouched...*Madre di Dio*, how do you do it? Not, you'll understand, that I am about to complain.'

41

Angelo...hot mistress material. Neither subject dovetailed. 'What are you d-doing in my hotel room?' she suddenly found the voice to demand explosively. 'How did you know that I would be here?'

'Ah, she speaks...shame,' Angelo sighed with mock regret. 'Now where do I start? This is not a hotel. It's a private house. It belongs to me. I came upon it three years ago when I was investing in Max's villa development. It was going to rack and ruin then but it was so totally private, I had to have it——'

'*Your house*?' Kelda repeated incredulously. 'This is your house? What the hell am I staying here for?'

'I brought you here,' Angelo said softly. 'It was astonishingly easy. Max St Saviour is a business acquaintance. He's very happily married and prone to romantic delusions. I had no problem persuading him to approach the Donaldson Agency on my behalf. He thought he was playing Cupid. Did you like the touch about the reduced fee? Now Max didn't like that bit but I felt it added a dash of authenticity...'

A slow, deep flush of almost uncontrollable rage was reddening Kelda's complexion. She couldn't even begin to believe what she was hearing, but there was something frighteningly sincere about the hard dark onslaught of Angelo's gaze. 'Are you telling me that there *is* no assignment...I don't believe you!' she snapped.

'Max couldn't afford you,' Angelo said with dulcet emphasis. 'But I can, and I don't need to know one end of a camera from another to know exactly what to do with you.'

Kelda's head was swimming with a mess of utterly bewildered thoughts. There *was* no assignment? Then why bring her here? Why would Angelo lure her to Tuscany? Why was Angelo surveying her as if she was a cream cake and he was starving for a bite to eat? Angelo had never looked at her like that before... and all the *double entendres*...what on earth was going on? Had Angelo gone insane? This was not Angelo as she knew him. This was another Angelo entirely.

'You really are the most spectacularly beautiful creature,' Angelo murmured in a thickened undertone. 'And if you stay in that bed much longer, I'm likely to join you.'

Kelda wrenched the sheet so high it came adrift from the foot of the mattress and exposed her bare feet, but she didn't notice. She couldn't take her eyes off Angelo's darkly handsome features. 'W-what are you talking about?' she demanded in a near shriek. 'Have you gone crazy?'

Angelo winced at the ear-splitting decibels. 'I wish I had volume control on your voice.'

'Y-you brought me here...all the way to Italy for an assignment that doesn't exist,' she recounted, spitting out each work with clarity. 'What I want to know is *why*?'

'I have this feeling that our mutual parents will get on much more happily with *you* out of the way,' Angelo drawled. 'I could quite happily have knocked you on the head and dragged you out of your apartment by the hair forty-eight hours ago. But that would have been foolish. And, *cara*, I am very rarely foolish——'

'You are right out of your tiny mind!' she launched at him in seething bewilderment.

'No. If you had simply disappeared, questions would have been asked,' he pointed out speciously. 'This way you're here on a perfectly respectable alibi——'

'But I won't be here for long! And you're going to pay for this!' Kelda spat.

'I have your passport, your money and your credit cards...not much use, those, are they?' Angelo remarked silkily. 'You're right up to your limit on all of them.'

'You have my passport...how do you *know* I'm up to my limit?' she suddenly heard herself demanding.

'I am completely conversant with your financial status,' Angelo admitted unashamedly. 'And I have to say, in my capacity as a banker, how did you get yourself in such a mess? You are in debt to the tune of thousands!'

Abruptly she turned her head away, utterly humiliated that Angelo of all people should know such things. She had been foolish with her money when she'd first started earning. But when Daisy had divorced Tomaso and had, inconceivably, refused to accept any alimony from him, Kelda had been determined to buy her mother a decent home to live in again.

She had bought Daisy a lovely little cottage not too far from London. It had not come cheap. She had sent her mother off on holiday several times. She had settled her brother's debts times without number, bought expensive presents for her family and friends. Her apartment had been the only major item she had ever bought for herself. It had never occurred to her that the gravy-train of her high income could come to a sudden frightening halt. But it had and she just hadn't been prepared for it.

'You really do *need* a rich patron, who can settle your debts and pick up the tab for your expensive tastes...someone who would never question the bills,' Angelo murmured with the soft, smooth delivery of a devil's advocate. 'I'm very generous with my lovers...I've never had a mistress before...you see, strange as it may seem to you *cara*...I've never had to buy a woman before. But the more I look at you in that bed and contemplate total possession and title, the more I see your investment potential...'

A steel band of tension was throbbing unbearably round her temples and it tightened another painful notch every time Angelo spoke. Perhaps she was very, very stupid but she just couldn't grasp why Angelo was behaving the way he was. 'I don't kn-know you like this,' she confided without meaning to.

Angelo vented a grim laugh that ironically made her feel much more at home with him. 'How could you? Much has changed over the past six years. Does it surprise you to learn that I deeply resented being forced to take responsibility for you when you became my stepsister?'

'Nobody asked you to take responsibility for me!' Kelda slung at him.

Angelo dealt her an assessing glance. 'But there was nobody else to do it. Our parents were abroad so much. And I know for a fact that my father was more than happy to leave you to me,' he continued drily. 'Daisy was such an adoring mother that he didn't want to get into trouble with her for disciplining you. And he would have done, make no mistake. Daisy's very protective of you. So I got landed with the job nobody else would touch!'

'How dare you say that?' Kelda threw at him fierily. 'How dare you?'

'And you were the most totally obnoxious teenager,' Angelo volunteered. 'You put me off having children for life.'

'If that means that there'll never be a junior edition of you running about making someone's life hell, I'm delighted to hear it!' But although the ready words flowed from her tongue, Kelda was dismayed to realise that she was deeply and genuinely hurt by what he had thrown at her. And she couldn't understand why. Hadn't she always known that Angelo hated her?

The difference was, she appreciated, that it had never once crossed her mind to wonder how Angelo felt about having the burden of a teenager thrust on him. She had not considered that aspect of those years before, had dimly imagined that Angelo had taken over simply to be officious and unpleasant. And why hadn't she thought more deeply... because to have reflected more deeply would have forced her to acknowledge the truth of what Angelo had said. Daisy and Tomaso had been abroad a

great deal and Tim had been a quiet, self-contained boy,
quite content to be sent off to boarding school and given
plenty of pocket money in return for a lack of personal
attention.

'I was only twenty-one,' Angelo pointed out, having
ignored her childish response. 'And you were out of
control. Between them your mother and your sweet old
great-aunt had spoilt you rotten. Daisy, quite frankly,
couldn't cope with you. You are very different from her
in temperament.'

Kelda could feel tears burning behind her lowered
eyelids. She had never hated Angelo so much and yet
simultaneously, she had never felt so savaged. She found
herself remembering the loneliness of those years and
discovered that inexplicably, deep down inside, she must
once have had the vague conviction that to take charge
of her in the first place, Angelo must have had some
slight affection for her. How she could have thought that
and yet believed that he hated her at the same time was
no more clear to her than anything else since she had
arrived in Tuscany.

'I was more like your father than your stepbrother,'
Angelo mused with an oddly chilling quality. 'You don't
know me like this because in the past six years you have
become an adult and I can now treat you as one. You
wouldn't believe the pleasure that that freedom gives me.'

Kelda pressed both hands against her pale cheeks and
forced herself to look at him over her straining fingers.
'Why did you bring me here?' she demanded in a shaken
tone.

'Why?' Glittering dark eyes slid over the wild tangle
of red-gold hair veiling her shoulders in a torrent of curls
and lingered on the exquisite perfection of the triangular
face pointed at him. 'Are you really that dumb? Six years
ago you virtually destroyed my relationship with my
father——'

'I...I didn't mean to——' Kelda was shocked and
unprepared for the directness of that attack.

'The only woman ever to put one over on me was just eighteen,' Angelo spelt out. 'But no blushing virgin. You knew exactly what you were doing that night——'

'I *didn't*!' she protested.

'And it worked a treat,' Angelo breathed softly, black ice eyes holding distressed green with raw force of will. 'You waited until you heard Daisy and Tomaso come in and then you skipped into my room, knowing that they'd be surprised to find the party over and that Daisy's first stop would be your own bedroom. Finding you absent, my father was certain to come looking for me... and what did he discover?'

'It wasn't like that!' Kelda argued half an octave higher, appalled by what he was accusing her of. 'It wasn't planned!'

'On the contrary, it was beautifully plotted and carried out,' Angelo contradicted with satire. 'You had to keep me quiet about what I'd seen earlier in the evening, and what better way? You were paranoid, as it happens. I had no intention of sharing that sordid little scene with your mother.'

'If you hadn't touched me, nothing *could* have happened!' Kelda told him in a wild surge.

Angelo threw back his dark head and laughed with sardonic amusement. '*Cara*, this is Angelo you're talking to, not Daisy! You were standing over me in a minuscule see-through nightdress, eating me with your eyes. Up until that night, I was ashamed of the fact that I wanted you——'

'W-wanted me?' Her full attention pinned to him, Kelda sat up straighter again with a jerk that very nearly dislodged the sheet that was her only veil of modesty.

'You were like a thorn sinking deeper and deeper into my flesh.' Angelo angled a terrifyingly cold smile over her. 'Full marks for the pretence of innocence, but you knew, *cara*. In the cradle, you were as old as Eve. You knew that I wanted you and I've often wondered how it would have gone if I hadn't found you playing the whore so indiscreetly in the library that night. That really was remarkably careless of you——'

'Careless,' Kelda repeated, her mind fathoms deep in shock from what he was telling her, only he did not appear to accept that he was telling her anything she hadn't already known. But dear lord...dear lord, the past she had so recently recalled was assuming colours and depths and meanings that had previously been a mystery to her.

Angelo shot her a suspicious glance. Hard, narrowed, sharp. 'The only way I could have had you then was by marriage,' he delivered silkily. 'That was the price and it would have been one hell of a price to get you flat on your back on the nearest available bed...but I damned near paid it. I was prepared to wait for you to grow up. Now that is a surprise to you, isn't it?'

'Y-yes.' She was incapable of saying anything else.

'And the reason I'm telling you that six years after the event is that I don't want you to waste your time plotting and planning how to turn this little sojourn abroad into a trip to the nearest church,' he spelt out flatly. 'I will *never* marry you.'

'N-no,' Kelda agreed, feeling like someone taking part in a Salvador Dali dream sequence of spectacular complexity. Marriage and Angelo. She could truly put her hand on her heart and swear that such a prospect had never crossed her mind in her wildest imaginings.

'But I will make love to you as no man ever has before,' Angelo swore in a sizzling undertone that purred along her sensitive nerve-endings like bittersweet chocolate, inflaming her in all sorts of intimate places she had never dreamt were so susceptible. She couldn't take her eyes off him. She was magnetised by the most extraordinary excitement. It came from somewhere deep and dark inside her, some secret place, until that moment undiscovered even by herself.

'I have had six long years to think about how I intend to entertain you,' Angelo savoured with unrestrained eroticism. 'And I knew that this moment would come. When you sent me that *Vogue* cover, I knew that we were playing the same waiting game. There you were wearing a string of priceless emeralds and nothing else——'

'It only looked that w-way!' Kelda heard herself stammer.

He dug a lean brown hand into the pocket of his riding pants and tossed something almost negligently on the white sheet. 'They came from Cartier...I bought them.'

Her long, luxuriant lashes lifted and dropped again but the glorious string of matched emeralds separated by diamonds still lay like a river of glittering fire in the strong sunlight flooding through the windows. She could not resist touching them with a tremulous finger. She had not seen them in six years.

Angelo laughed, softly, lazily and with immense and unconcealed satisfaction, rampantly amused by her state of dazed, unspeaking paralysis. He strolled confidently round to the side of the bed, scooped up the necklace and sank down on the edge of the bed. He smoothed her torrent of hair gently out of his path and she felt the cool touch of his fingers at her nape, then the weight of the jewels at her throat, and she couldn't breathe, couldn't move, couldn't speak...

His breath fanned her cheek and her heartbeat thundered in her eardrums and still she couldn't move. He rearranged her hair with the intimacy of a lover, trailed a caressing forefinger down her knotted spine. 'So tense I could almost believe you were terrified,' he teased and then he pressed his mouth briefly, hungrily, agonisingly to an incredibly sensitive spot just below her right ear and she could feel every bone melt, every muscle give way in surrender.

'Tonight,' he breathed huskily, and vaulted gracefully upright again.

She began to shiver, suddenly cold, shock giving way to wave upon wave of after-shock.

'Do you want to come riding with me?' He was already at the door in two long, elegant strides. 'No? I'll meet you for breakfast in an hour in the courtyard.'

And then he was gone. Kelda slid bonelessly down the bed. She was in Tuscany with Angelo. Angelo wanted her. Angelo had apparently been lusting after her for years. Angelo was prepared to deck her in emeralds and diamonds before breakfast. Angelo was asking her...no, expecting her to become his mistress. Hot mistress material. And when he had touched her, it had been like coming alive in paradise...she had felt...she had felt wildly immoral and wonderfully sensual for the very first time in her chequered and, until now, not that exciting existence.

So much, for not being a *real* woman, she tasted. Angelo had actually admitted that he would have married her six years ago purely to satisfy his hunger for her. *Hunger*—she savoured the concept shamelessly. All this time and she hadn't known, hadn't even suspected that Angelo desired her. She rolled over on her stomach and stretched, conscious of every individual skin cell in her body. She felt incredibly powerful for several more minutes...this was Angelo where she had always wanted him...on his knees.

And then common sense began to assert itself. It was an uphill battle but it got there in the end, hacking a passage through the layers of sublime contentment that she was suddenly quite unable to reasonably explain. Did she like Angelo wanting her? Oh, yes. It was retribution for all he had put her through in the past.

But that was her teenage self talking, not the adult she was supposed to be. It was impossible to explain the fact that she had allowed him to festoon her in emeralds and diamonds unchecked. She put both hands to her throat in sudden anger and attempted to remove the necklace. Five fruitless minutes later, when she was afraid of breaking the wretched thing, she gave up and leapt off the bed, wide awake but still...she just couldn't help it...still not thinking straight.

Of course, she was going home on the first available plane. He had her passport but he would hardly insist on keeping it...would he? Dear heaven, he had virtually kidnapped her! He had lured her here with the intent of seduction. Such an old-fashioned word and quite inappropriate. The sole seduction Angelo intended to employ was his immense wealth.

You arrogant, conceited swine, she suddenly thought, livid. Angelo actually believed that all he had to do was flash extravagant jewellery at her and she would fall down gratefully at his feet. He had reminded her how broke she was. He was willing to strew the passage to his bed with emeralds, diamonds and cold, hard cash. Angelo might find her incredibly desirable and she really couldn't restrain the flush of heat that enveloped her at that repeated reflection but his confession had not been coined to flatter her. Angelo was treating her like a high-class whore.

What the hell sort of a spell had he cast, that she had lain there and simply listened without rearranging his features for him? Men had insulted her before, but leave it to Angelo to fathom out the grossest possible insult! He assumed that all he had to do was ask and he would receive...he really did think that! Abruptly, hot moisture flooded her eyes and she was shocked at herself.

She didn't know why she was crying. She ought to be laughing her head off. Angelo had miscalculated and made an ass of himself. She was not for sale, she was not tempted, and if she lusted after being badly treated and abused she would find a street corner to haunt faster than she would sink to the depravity of allowing Angelo Rossetti to lay one arrogant finger on her!

Six years...six years, though, he had waited for her, wanting her, thinking about her, presumably noticing her every time she appeared in the newspapers and on advertising hoardings and in glossy magazines. Six years—she just couldn't get that out of her mind. Six years... good to know that she hadn't been the only one scanning boring newsprint, gossip columns, tuning in to BBC 2 when there was a stock-market crisis, just *knowing* he'd be interviewed...

And why had she done that, she asked herself in sudden stricken dismay? A sliver of conversation she had had recently with Tim returned to her.

'Did you see Angelo holding forth on TV last night?' she had mocked.

'I don't watch that sort of stuff.' Tim had dismissed. 'Sometimes I think you're obsessed with Angelo...'

'Because I hate him,' she had responded drily.

Was that a kind of obsession too? Was hatred so all-encompassing? And, if she hated him, why hadn't she broken out into a rash of revulsion when he'd pressed his mouth to the pulse beneath her ear?

She turned the shower on full blast on cold. Go on admit it, she scorned with throbbing self-disgust. Ever since that night, Angelo has fascinated you. He had taught her the meaning of desire. A terrifying devastation of the senses. After that night, she had decided she was a slut in the making, all rampant hormones and no self-control. She had imagined that Angelo would recall her response to him with cruel amusement.

She had cringed from the memory. She had hidden from the fact that even though hours earlier she had been subjected to a brutal assault of a very sexual nature, she had still contrived to melt into Angelo's arms without a shred of fear. He had stolen her peace of mind forever. He had shown her how frail she was under fire of her own sensuality. But only with him... only with him, a little voice whispered inside her head. Only with Angelo.

Admit it: *you want him too*. Incredibly bad taste, she told herself. It was purely physical chemistry, the sort of thing she had no control over. But of course, she would have complete control of that weakness now because she had freely admitted it to herself. As an arrangement of flesh, muscle and bones, Angelo was indisputably very nicely arranged. However, that was *all* it was, just a stupid, mindless physical thing.

Having placed Angelo exactly where he belonged, Kelda got dressed in a pair of matador-style high waisted cotton trousers and a sheer lace shirt. Combing out her towel-dried hair, she didn't even bother to reach for her cosmetics case. After all, she didn't want Angelo imagining that she was making an effort for his benefit! Poor Angelo, she reflected, feeling much more like herself. This time, he really had gone in over his head!

'My passport, please,' she rehearsed in front of the mirror, and laughed.

There was no sign of breakfast in the courtyard she had entered the night before. She trekked back through the echoing hall, glancing into rooms on her passage past, her feet moving more and more slowly. Fabulous house, she found herself thinking, more of a *palazzo* than a mere dwelling. Trust Angelo to have found it, she thought. Probably picked it up for a song and then spent millions on it which he could well afford, she conceded darkly, absently fingering the emeralds still at her throat. But where, oh, where were the serfs to people his feudal kingdom in the Tuscan hills ... impossible to imagine Angelo 'doing' for himself!

There was a little inner courtyard. There he was, bathed in a pool of golden sunshine that glinted off his ebony-dark hair, accentuated his strong profile and turned his gorgeous eyes to honey-gold. Something went hip-hippety-hop behind her breastbone and she momentarily froze on the threshold. All of a sudden, as he looked at her, it was so incredibly hard to breathe. It was intimidating.

He slid upright. Superb manners, she absently recalled. Angelo was the only male she had ever met capable of opening a door and standing back politely for you to precede him even in the middle of a violent argument.

'I want my passport,' she announced.

'Have some cappuccino,' Angelo suggested smoothly.

She planted both hands on her slim hips. 'Look, the comedy is over, Angelo. I want my passport.'

'No.'

Kelda waited. 'Is that it? Is that all you think you have to say? *No*? And the little woman says sorry for asking!'

'You signed the usual contract with St Saviour Villas?'

Kelda frowned. It had come over by special messenger within hours of Ella's call. 'Yes, but the contract was a blind——'

'I can assure you that Max will stand by it if I ask him to,' Angelo murmured softly. 'It would be your word against his that there was never an assignment in the first place. I would ensure that he sued you for breaking the contract. He would say that you had walked out. Can you afford to be sued for default right now?'

Her lips had parted in disbelief. 'You couldn't do that!'

'I never threaten what I can't deliver. Think about it . . . you return to London, inform the agency that you were—what?'

'Blasted well lured out here by a crackpot and his accomplice in crime!' Kelda shot at him in outrage.

'I do believe my reputation and my influence would upstage yours, *cara*. Who would believe such a thing of me?'

Kelda couldn't credit what she was hearing. 'I would believe it!' she shrieked tempestuously.

'But it is scarcely credible that I, Angelo Rossetti, would go to such lengths to entrap a woman——' he countered with silky emphasis.

Kelda stared at him with wide furiously frustrated eyes. She wanted so badly to hit him, she didn't trust herself to get any closer. Her nails dug into her palms.

'You see *cara*...my reputation is considerably more...shall we say...clean than yours?' Angelo added in offensive addition.

'You lousy, rotten, calculating bastard!' she hissed.

He offered her a fresh roll as she collapsed down into a seat opposite him. Her knees had given way. She took a deep breath. 'Angelo, you wouldn't do that——'

'But I wouldn't be doing it. I would be safely behind the scenes, quietly pulling the strings,' he responded gently. 'Did you really think that I brought you here without covering myself on all fronts?'

Half an hour ago, she had felt rather like a fluffy lamb gambolling on a deep, lush and grassy meadow. It had been a game. All of it. A glorious and exciting game that challenged her. But now, she was feeling sick and shaky. Angelo was making it indisputably clear that the kind of game he liked to play had suicidally high stakes.

'This...this Max St Saviour,' she framed, 'why would he lie for you?'

A hint of a smile curved his ruthlessly sensual mouth. 'He couldn't afford not to lie if I told him to——'

'Hell's teeth!' Kelda exclaimed in horror. 'You don't mean that you would put pressure on the poor man simply to punish me!'

Angelo sipped at his coffee with inhuman calm. 'I should dislike the necessity,' he conceded very softly. 'But to cover my own back? Yes, I would do it. In a tight corner I always come out fighting. One cannot be sentimental about the weapons one employs.'

'I'll go to my mother, tell her everything!' Kelda threatened wildly.

'And she'll think you've suffered a resurgence of your infatuation with me and been cruelly rejected,' Angelo inputted sardonically. 'And she will be terribly, terribly upset on your behalf——'

'My m-mother knows me better than that!' Kelda swore, her cheeks flaming with outraged colour. 'I was never infatuated with you!'

'We know that,' he said lazily. 'But does she?

Kelda tugged with shaking fingers at the clasp of the necklace. Suddenly it felt like it was strangling her. 'Take this bloody thing off me *now*!' she demanded.

'It has a trick fastening for security.'

'I'll break it!'

'You value beauty too much to destroy it.' Angelo lifted a careless hand and stroked an amused forefinger along the tremulous line of her generous mouth. 'And so do I,' he murmured in a wine dark undertone of intimacy. 'You really must stop underestimating me, *cara*. It's such a waste of your energies.'

Kelda jerked violently away from the taunting caress and left the table.

CHAPTER FOUR

STANDING on the stone balcony, Kelda drained her cup of cappuccino and moodily surveyed the incredibly beautiful countryside spread out like a picturesque map. When Angelo had said 'totally private', he had not been joking. A patchwork of wheat and barley fields, grape and olive groves and copses of trees was interrupted by the sienna walls and terracotta roofs of occasional farmhouses. There was no town anywhere that she could see within walking distance.

And what would she do even if there was a town? Offer herself up to the local policeman? Refusing to give up her passport had to be a crime, but did she really want to try to prove such a claim against a native Italian like Angelo, who was undoubtedly a major landowner in the locality and probably held in considerable respect? She would end up with egg on her face.

She could not risk being sued for defaulting on her contract. Her relations with Ella Donaldson were poor right now. If she was sued, she would get the name of being unreliable as well as being notorious, she reflected grimly, and she might never work again. Photographic modelling was a tough business and behind her, ready to walk over her and take her place, were countless beautiful, ambitious teenage girls eager for their chance of success. Tim had called her famous but she was not in the super-model bracket, although her career had been heading that way before Danny Philips had tripped her up.

Like it or not, Angelo had her trapped. She could hitch her passage to the nearest embassy and say she had lost her passport but she would be in breach of contract if she walked out. Ella wouldn't be a sympathetic listener

to some far-fetched story about Max St Saviour and
Angelo Rossetti.

She was here for only two days...what could happen
in two days? Angelo was enjoying wielding power over
her. Well, let him, she urged herself. Up to a point,
anyway. Angelo wanted revenge for that night six years
ago. This was it. Now that she was prepared, she could
take Angelo in her stride, couldn't she? Beyond keeping
her here as an unwilling guest, he couldn't force her to
do anything that she didn't want to do.

He had had breakfast sent up to her on a tray. It had
been delivered by not one but two giggling maids, intent
on getting a good look at Angelo's latest bit of fluff.
Her chin came up. Why should she care about what the
staff thought? Nobody else was ever likely to know that
she had even been here.

She strolled downstairs and paused in the doorway of
the room Angelo evidently used as an office. It was so
painfully well-organised and tidy, it screamed Angelo,
and unexpectedly she found herself smiling, imagining
him seated behind that exquisitely polished desk. Angelo
wanted her. Imagine that...Angelo, sitting back to wait
for her to stumble and fall into his ruthless hands.
Angelo, who had probably never had to wait for any
woman and who would, sadly for him, still be waiting
for her on Judgement Day!

'You look very pleased with yourself.'

Kelda spun and very nearly tripped on the corner of
a rug. Angelo raised his hands to steady her, long brown
fingers curving round her forearms. Without warning,
he was much too close for comfort. 'You can let me go
now,' she said breathlessly. 'I'm not liable to fall at your
feet——'

'Ever?' Lustrous eyes of gold challenged her with assurance. 'Don't be so sure, *cara*.'

'Of that I am very sure.' But her breath shortened in
her throat as his scrutiny wandered at an outrageously
leisurely pace over her, lingering unashamedly on the

proud swell of her breasts. In shocking betrayal, her nipples tightened and thrust forward against the fine lace fabric, heat pooling between her thighs.

Kelda pulled back, crossing her arms protectively over herself. She couldn't believe that he could make her react like that without even touching her. Her body trembled, taut and sensitive, on the brink of arousal. And it had happened so fast. She was shattered by the discovery that her body had a life of its own in Angelo's vicinity.

A slow, sensual smile tilted his beautiful mouth but surprisingly he said nothing. He hadn't noticed, she told herself in relief.

'Would you like to go out to lunch?'

'I'm allowed out?' she prompted in astonishment.

'You're not in a prison cell . . . or a cage,' he added with something less than his usual cool, and she noticed the strangest thing. Dark colour had overlaid his tautened cheekbones when he made that crack about a cell.

A slight pleat formed between her brows, for she had no idea why he had suddenly tensed. 'I'd love to go out,' she murmured truthfully.

'So tell me about Jeff Maitland,' Angelo invited as he raked the Porsche down the dusty hillside. 'I hear that he wants to marry you.'

'Surprised?' Kelda tossed back, eyeing him from behind her sunglasses.

'Not at all, *cara*. But I suspect his father might have something to say about it . . .' Angelo drawled and then continued speciously, 'Of course, perhaps you've already met Maitland Senior?'

Kelda compressed her lips, stayed silent.

'He's a narrow-minded prig,' Angelo proffered smoothly. 'And he's been telling anyone willing to listen recently that he wants you out of his son's life.'

Hot pink flamed in her cheeks.

'Now, I am not a narrow-minded prig,' Angelo divulged softly. 'I can live with absolutely *anything* that you might choose to tell me about your past.'

Her teeth clenched but she turned her head and cast him a glimmering smile. 'I don't kiss and tell, *caro*.'

'But your lovers do,' Angelo inputted flatly.

Kelda stiffened. 'I bet you devoured every word!' she condemned.

'Yes but I don't say that I believed every word of it,' he pointed out drily. 'Of course, if you want me to tie you up and cover you with whipped cream, I'm more than willing... but on a first date?'

'I *love* strawberries and cream,' Kelda asserted, aggressively determined not to plead her innocence on any count.

'Cream is so messy... I prefer champagne,' Angelo countered huskily, rather taking the wind out of her sails. 'Now, the black leather and the riding crop. I didn't credit that. That made me laugh, most inconveniently in the middle of a very boring meeting. You are not a sadist——'

'But I feel very sadistic around you, Angelo,' Kelda told him, her eyes glittering furiously at him.

'You'll purr like a cat in my bed,' Angelo murmured silkily. 'And you won't need black leather, zebra skins or jacuzzis to enliven the experience.'

'Dream on,' Kelda spelt out shakily. 'I will never get into your bed!'

'You are more likely not to want to get out of it again.'

'You don't suffer much in the way of humility, do you, Angelo?'

'Not in the bedroom, no,' he conceded silkily.

Kelda took a deep breath. 'And the idea that I have had dozens of lovers doesn't even bother you?'

'It might if I believed that... but I don't.'

Kelda was sharply disconcerted. 'You don't?'

'A woman who has had dozens of sexual partners wouldn't get all hot and bothered talking about sex. She

wouldn't blush when I looked at her breasts, either,'
Angelo delineated with immense calm, and then shot her
a nakedly amused glance that sent her pulse racing. 'In
the space of a couple of hours, I've learnt more about
you by observation than you could begin to imagine.'

'Really?' she endeavoured to sound bored but deep
down inside she was churning up with dismay.

'Really,' Angelo confirmed lazily.

He took her to a tiny sleepy village on a hill. It was
entirely enclosed by pale thirteenth-century walls and half
a dozen lookout towers. The restaurant was in a former
monastery and they chose to dine outside below the
spreading shade of a giant chestnut tree. Kelda accepted
a glass of wine and stood at the wall, taking in the spectacular view of the wooded valley far below. It was a
truly glorious day and the world seemed to be drowsing
in the noon day heat. Behind her, Angelo was choosing
their meal with the sort of serious selectivity that made
her smile.

'You know,' she heard herself saying without really
thinking about it, 'I wasn't going to interfere between
my mother and your father.'

'But you already have,' Angelo countered drily.

'I was asked for my opinion and I gave it.' Kelda
shrugged. 'What was wrong with that?'

'Apart from the fact that Daisy is highly suggestible
and very much afraid of damaging her relationship with
you, what makes you think that your opinion was worth
hearing?' Angelo murmured very quietly. 'You have all
the sensitivity of a steel butterfly in your own relationships with men——'

'I beg your pardon?' Kelda demanded hotly.

'And you've never been with any man longer than
about six weeks. I would say you were uniquely un-
qualified to offer advice on affairs of the heart——'

'A steel butterfly?' she queried acidly.

'I both heard and saw you in action with young
Maitland.'

'He was being difficult,' she parried uncomfortably.

'So you went home alone and left him drowning his sorrows. Your heart really bleeds, *cara*,' Angelo mocked.

'He wants to marry me and I don't want to marry him. A bleeding heart would have been out of place.' Kelda held his lustrous dark gold eyes in angry challenge. 'How do you dump your women when you're finished with them, Angelo?'

'Not in a public place,' he parried quietly. 'And they invariably see the writing on the wall in advance and extract themselves with dignity.'

Kelda flushed, uneasily aware that she had been clumsy with Jeff. Her mouth tightened. Just like old times. Angelo criticising her, implying that she did not have a great deal of class. It was a relief to see the waiter approaching them across the cobbles.

The meal began with a salad of young turkey and grapefruit and was followed by rosettes of veal with artichoke sauce. She refused the saffron rice with quail and drank glass after glass of wine in a vain attempt to cool down in the heat before falling victim to the *spongata*, a very rich pastry filled with walnuts, almonds, pine nuts and raisins mixed with cognac and honey.

'I do believe I have found food I would kill for,' she sighed, blissfully stuffed as she rested back in her chair.

'I didn't think you would eat most of it,' Angelo confided.

'I lost so much weight last month, I can afford to indulge a little.' Pleasantly relaxed, Kelda asked him a question that had been bothering her for several days. 'Tell me, when did you change your mind about my mother? What makes you so keen for her to marry your father again?'

'He hasn't been happy since the divorce. He was working too hard...in spite of medical advice. Hence the heart attack,' Angelo divulged unemotionally. 'He still loves your mother. To be brutally honest, even if she was the money-grabbing blonde I once thought she was, I'd still encourage the marriage. He needs her. I accidentally walked in on them the first time she came to the hospital and there she was, fluffing up his pillows, hanging on his every word, generally looking at him as if he was a god come down from Olympus——'

Kelda could not avoid wincing at the description of her mother's behaviour around Tomaso. 'I bet he loved it——'

'Fifteen minutes of Daisy and he was itching to get out of that bed,' Angelo said wryly. 'She made him feel like a man again. She did more for him than all the specialists I had flown in to try and cheer him up about his future prospects.'

Kelda chewed at her lower lip. 'Mum can't help being like that round a man,' she muttered defensively. 'She's the nurturing, cherishing type.'

'I have to admit that when I first saw her in action years ago, I thought it was all an act.' Angelo topped up her empty glass and sent her a shimmering smile that made her feel oddly dizzy. 'Of course, it wasn't. It was just Daisy. I know that now. She's one of that rare breed, loving and giving...no greed, no calculation. Eleven years ago, I should have had greater faith in my father's judgement. He's no fool.'

Kelda's entire attention was intently pinned to him. A glorious smile spontaneously curved her full mouth. The free admission that he had entirely misjudged her mother, followed by such generous praise of Daisy's nature, soothed once raw loyalties and delighted her no end. In response to her smile, Angelo's intense charm blazed forth, catching her unawares.

Feeling scorched, her heart leaping behind her breastbone in a sudden onrush of excitement, she lowered her lashes and struggled to think of something to say but Angelo got in first.

'What was your father like?'

Bemusedly, she repeated, 'My *father*?' She was so unused to anyone mentioning her father and then once more, she smiled. 'He was really wonderful,' she said softly.

Dense ebony lashes dropped low on Angelo's intent gaze. 'Tell me about him,' he encouraged very quietly.

'I get my height and my colouring from him,' Kelda shared with unhidden pride. 'He was hot-tempered but he had a terrific sense of humour and he was marvellous with kids. I remember the way he used to play with us when we were very young. He was like a child himself sometimes.' She laughed. 'We moved house a lot. He was very restless, or maybe it was Mum who was restless. He started working abroad when I was five...it really broke my heart——'

Angelo seemed strangely preoccupied with the contents of his glass. 'Where abroad?' he cut in.

'He was an oil worker with a big company in Jordan.'

'Jordan?' Angelo repeated softly. 'Did he come home very often after he started working in...Jordan?'

She frowned. 'It cost so much, you see. He came back a couple of times but we really kept in touch by letter. I have every letter that he ever wrote to me. He used to tell me terrific stories about the desert. Savage Arabs and crazy camels. He had a great imagination...I dare say he made up half of it to amuse me——'

'Possibly,' Angelo murmured in a curiously flat tone.

Kelda didn't notice. 'It's silly, but I always used to wish that he would write direct to me instead of just enclosing his letter to me in with one to Mum. She used to bring them to Liverpool when she came, and she never brought the envelopes with the foreign stamps and I always wanted those to show off to my friends!'

Silence had fallen. A bee buzzed languorously over to the acacia blossoms by the side of the wall. Kelda was feeling wonderfully relaxed. 'What hurt most,' she sighed, 'was only finding out that he had died *after* the funeral! Mum thought we were too young to handle it but I was thirteen and I still remember her coming up to Liverpool to tell us. I was so angry with her for not telling me immediately.'

'She was trying to protect you.' Angelo rose with that lethal elegance of movement that was so characteristic of him. 'I think it's time to go.'

Kelda reddened. 'You should have said that you were bored.' She was furious with herself for rabbiting on as she had. Why had she done that? She had never discussed her father with anybody before.

'You never bore me, *cara*.'

As she clashed with his brilliant dark eyes, she felt oddly naked, horribly vulnerable all of a sudden. Abruptly, she stood up and their surroundings swam dizzily around them. She had had far too much wine. Alcohol loosened the tongue, she reflected ruefully. Angelo closed a large hand over her smaller one and silently guided her down the steep steps to the car.

Her stupid fingers were clumsy with the seatbelt. Brushing them away, Angelo did it up for her. 'Do you still think of me as a slum chid?' she heard herself ask without forethought.

Lean fingers curved to her delicate jawbone, inexorably forcing her to turn her head towards him. 'Shut up,' he said softly, not unkindly.

'I did grow up on a council estate——' she began sharply.

'I told you to shut up.' His brown fingers moved caressingly over her taut cheekbone and then he leant down, deftly winding his other hand into her hair and let the tip of his tongue slowly and smoothly trace the tremulous line of her lower lip.

Her breath escaped with a tiny gasp and her heart thudded like that of a wild bird in a cage. She wanted his mouth so badly she burned, every sense pitched to an unbearable high as he toyed expertly with the sensitive fullness he had discovered. Her eyes slid shut, her

long throat arching as she bent back her head
instinctively.

Angelo set her back from him and fired the engine of
the car. Her lashes swept up on glazed green eyes, her
whole body throbbing with an intensity that was pure
pain.

A blunt forefinger raked down the slender length of
her thigh. 'I know,' Angelo breathed thickly.

Kelda looked out of the side window, fighting for
composure. She saw two elderly women, dressed in
black, crossing the empty square towards the tiny church.
But they didn't seem real. The only reality she could
currently register was the seething sexual vibrations in
the atmosphere.

And she couldn't handle the silence that lay between
them. Deliberately she rested her head back on the re-
straint and pretended to doze. The second the Porsche
raked to a halt in the courtyard, she leapt out of it. She
couldn't get away from him quickly enough.

'Kelda.'

Involuntarily, she found herself glancing back. 'I'm
going for a walk.'

'Fine.' Angelo held her strained scrutiny with unnerving ease and tenacity. He was in control. The raw
masculine power of him sprang out at her. Angelo, a
predator and a sensualist combined. She had let her
guard down over lunch and it had not only been the
wine. Angelo had drawn her out with subtle skill and
she had fallen for it, talking her foolish head off about
her father. A man, who had been little more than an
unskilled labourer on an oil site, a man in whom Angelo
could not have the slightest genuine interest, though he
had admirably concealed the fact, she conceded bitterly.

He strolled over to her. 'The gardens are rather
wild——'

'I don't mind.'

'But beautiful in an informal style,' he completed.
She abandoned hope of shaking him off.

'You're like a fox waiting for the hounds to come in for the kill,' Angelo remarked silkily as they descended the terrace steps, passing beds blazing with a mixture of perennials and wild flowers.

It wasn't a bad comparison, but that he should openly make it outraged her pride. She snatched in air headily weighted with the scent of flowers and moved on in the direction of a rioting shrubbery.

'You invite only weak, inadequate men to your bed,' Angelo drawled. 'That way you stay in control, and that's very important to you, Kelda. Isn't it?'

'I find you incredibly offensive!' she flared incredulously.

'If you haven't had much loyalty from your lovers, you can only blame yourself.' Angelo dealt her furious hectically flushed face a chillingly amused glance. 'Inadequate men boast and tell whoppers in news-print——'

'Or sore losers!' Kelda threw back, still walking at top speed, but the ground was descending steeply now and she was forced to slow down.

'If it's not too rude a question,' Angelo murmured smoothly, 'how many of them *were* losers?'

She whirled round and just exploded. Lifting her hand, she slapped him so hard across one hard cheekbone that her whole arm went numb, and then the pain came. She had hurt her wrist and she bent over, pressing it into her stomach, sucking in oxygen in a strangled gasp.

'I *could* say it served you right.' Angelo reached out for her arm and cradled her wrist between surprisingly gentle hands. His fingers explored her fine bones. She didn't look at him, she stared fixedly at the grass until it blurred. 'You've wrenched it, that's all. Relax, *cara*...I'm not about to hit you back but I should warn you that I have a very hot temper. I lose it rarely but, when I do, sensible individuals dive for the nearest shelter.'

He released her hand. Her throat was closing over. Tears were threatening. Her emotions were storming about in all directions. 'You can dump the Mr Nice Guy routine!' she advised unsteadily. 'I hate you, Angelo. I have always hated you. That's what makes your ambition to seduce me into your bed so *laughable*!'

'I could have screwed you in the Porsche with an audience of shocked pensioners, and all without one word of seduction,' Angelo delivered with brutal candour.

Kelda jerked and flinched as though he had punched her in the stomach. She forced her head up, was literally nailed to the spot by the fierce anger flaming in his golden eyes. 'No...' she whispered in feverish, desperate denial.

'And what does seduce mean?' Angelo wasn't finished with her yet. 'To deceive? I have been totally honest with you. To corrupt? The days of your innocence are long gone. Once I would have put a wedding-ring on your finger before I touched you. I would have treated you with honour and respect——'

'Stop it!' She fled into the orchard of peach and cherry trees, frantic to escape that mercilessly cruel tongue.

She didn't get very far before a powerful hand closed over one slim shoulder and yanked her back. He spun her round with frightening strength. 'Look at me!' he demanded with inborn arrogance, glittering dark eyes scanning her pale, distraught face. 'Your freedom is gone, and not only now, *cara*. It's gone for as long as I want you. I will keep you and I will clothe you and you will not make a single move that you haven't cleared with me first. You are *mine* and you had better start adjusting to that idea fast. I am not the most patient of men.'

Shaking all over, Kelda sucked in great gulps of oxygen. She was devastated by what he had said. Every lancing syllable rang with savage confidence. 'You can't take my freedom a-away——'

'But I already have,' he reminded her. 'And this is only the beginning.'

'You can do nothing to m-me,' she persisted, fighting sheer cold threat to the last bastion of her strength. 'Talk's cheap!'

He stared down at her and then released his breath in a slow hiss. 'It doesn't have to be like this *cara*. You can't fight me and win. Surrender would be so much sweeter for both of us. Capitulate with grace and you will discover how generous I can be——'

'I can live without emeralds and d-diamonds from Cartier,' she had to force the assurance past her convulsed throat.

'But I don't think you can live without me.' Angelo said with velvet clarity.

Kelda went white and then red, functioning on the most basic of responses. What she felt was pretty much what she thought. And what she felt was cold, hard fear followed by a sudden flaring surge of sexual awareness so intense that her whole body heated.

'You need me——'

'No,' she argued fierily, 'never. I have never needed any man.'

Angelo was unimpressed. He curved a lean hand almost negligently to her taut spinal cord. 'Until me,' he countered thickly, his lean, lithe body tensing against hers as her tongue snaked out to moisten her dry lips. 'And I haven't even kissed you yet . . .'

'Let go, Angelo,' she said breathlessly.

'I think I will.' His stunning eyes skimmed with hungry sensuality over her and then he drew her close with controlled power and took her mouth with slow, drugging intensity.

She was a good strong swimmer but she drowned in Angelo's arms. Six years melted away and she was back, back where her body told her she belonged, back where the world contracted into the crazy thunder of her heart and the mad race of the hot blood in her veins. A sensation akin to a hot wire being jerked tight knifed through her stomach, and with a stifled moan she arched her back in response to a pleasure than was close to pain.

Angelo said something rough in Italian and he was tugging her down in the lush meadow grass. The two buttons on her back that secured her top came adrift, fabric drifting down her arms over her wrists in a soft whisper, and all the time he was making love to her mouth with a naked and devouring passion that excited her to the brink of madness. Her fingers were dug deep in the springy depths of his hair, tracing the shape of his head, luxuriating in the silky strands, holding him to her.

He pulled her hands away and lifted his mouth from hers and then he just looked at her, a feverish flush of colour accentuating his striking cheekbones, his breathing pattern audibly fractured.

Her breasts were small, high and perfectly formed. Her nipples were shamelessly distended rose-pink buds. Angelo released his breath in a long, sighing groan as though he was afraid to touch her. She knelt there in front of him, quivering all over, every heated inch of her flesh ready to take fire.

The silence was electric. A voracious hunger vibrated like a physical aura between them. 'If I touch you . . . do you vanish?' Angelo whispered unsteadily.

'Do you?' Without any need for thought to precipitate the action, she leant forward and all fingers and thumbs embarked on unbuttoning his silk shirt. When it was open, he trailed it off with scant ceremony.

She looked at him exactly as he looked at her: with a driven, utterly consuming absorption. She dragged passion-glazed eyes possessively over the bronzed breadth of his muscular chest. A tangle of rough dark curls clung damply to his golden skin, arrowing down into a silky furrow over his flat, hard stomach.

She couldn't swallow, she couldn't move, but she had never wanted so badly to touch another human being.

It was a fire in her blood more potent and more powerful than any fever. Angelo reached for her in the same moment that she was about to reach for him. He hauled her on to his hard thighs and shaped her breasts with his hands. A stifled cry was dredged from her as he caught her nipples between thumb and forefinger and gently pulled on them.

She had not known that she would be so incredibly sensitive there that one touch and her whole body would become one gigantic yearning ache. But Angelo must have known by instinct.

'You are so glorious,' Angelo murmured against the corner of her lips. 'So perfect...*bella, mia cara.*'

His passionate mouth took hers and she shuddered with excitement as his clever fingers toyed with her swollen flesh. Nothing existed but the urgent, increasingly desperate hunger of her body to be submerged in his. He lifted her up as though she was a doll, unzipped her trousers, effortlessly peeled them away. Then he closed his hands over the ripe swell of her hips and buried his mouth hotly against her breasts.

It was electrifying. Her fingernails dug unwittingly into his broad shoulders as he licked and stroked and tantalised her to the edge of insanity. His hand cupped the apex of her thighs, his fingers splaying firmly against the damp scrap of silk and lace that was all that separated him from her.

'You are mine,' Angelo told her, lowering her into the grass with raw determination. 'Tell me that, before I bury myself in that exquisite body...'

Her lashes lifted. She focused on blazing golden eyes and melted to the consistency of honey all in one go. 'Yours,' she framed in a whisper of sound torn from the very depths of her.

'Always,' Angelo attached with savage emphasis.

Her desire for him was so powerful, he could have made her say anything, do anything in that instant but then the outside world intervened. She heard the low mutter of male voices, a soft burst of laughter and she went rigid.

'Gently, *cara*,' Angelo soothed. 'We're behind a twenty-foot wall.'

Shaken up, Kelda stared up at him in sudden torment. Beyond him she saw the peach and cherry trees, and mental awareness returned. For a split-second, still agonisingly controlled by her aching body, she wished it away again. She wanted him so much, she wanted to die if she couldn't have him. And she knew then without any helpful prompting from him what feeling suicidal felt like.

She knew then why she had always been afraid of Angelo. Why Angelo, alone of all men, threatened her peace of mind. You took fascination and obsession and a devastating physical desire and whatever the recipe produced, it was *not* hatred.

Through heavily lidded eyes Angelo dealt her an oblique look, the hard planes of his strong features shuttered. He reached for her discarded top and was smoothly feeding her arms into it before she grasped that, while she had been wildly out of control and lost to all reason, Angelo had never planned, it seemed, to consummate his desire for her in a peach and cherry orchard.

Had it been a punishment for calling that desire *laughable*? She turned cold and shivered. In anguish, she relived the torrid abandonment of her response to him. She didn't feel like laughing. Fear fluttered in her throat and churned in her stomach. She was not as tough as she had thought she was. Angelo had shot down that illusion in flames.

With supreme self-assurance, Angelo reached down a lean hand and hauled her upright. Kelda trailed her fingers free in violent rejection. Her brain was working now at a furious rate. Nothing that Angelo had so far threatened her with was worth this humiliation! Tonight, somehow, some way, no matter what it took, she was leaving . . .

CHAPTER FIVE

KELDA had only brought one dress, fashionably floral, ankle-length and buttoned from scoop neckline to hem. She had packed it because it was casual and un-crushable. Her fingers fluttered tautly towards the glittering jewels still encircling her throat. People put collars on dogs to control them, and after the collar came the lead ... it was all part of the training. Pure rage glittered in her emerald-green eyes. Later she would break the necklace. It certainly wasn't going with her!

The high of fury and self-loathing powering her had yet to dissipate. She had degraded herself. She had been a fully participating partner in Angelo's arms. Her skin burned as she recalled how he had made her feel, how she had behaved. There was no excuse. She was not a teenager at the mercy of rampaging hormones. She was a grown woman, supposedly in control of her own responses.

Dear heaven, she had *actually* thought that she had a fairly low sex drive. So many men had tried and failed to rouse her to passion. Her distaste for intimacy had been intense. She had blamed Angelo for her apparent frigidity. He had treated her appallingly that night six years ago. She had been at a very sensitive age when Angelo had contrived to combine sex, shame and sleaze all into one uneasy package inside her impressionable mind.

But what infuriated her most of all was that none of those inhibitions had prevented her from responding wildly to Angelo. It was sexual infatuation ... what else could it be? A raw physical attraction of the lowest order. That Angelo had known that he could exercise such power over her, long before she herself even suspected

73

it, was doubly humiliating. On that level, her own lack of experience made her a pitifully easy target and no way... absolutely no way was she sticking around for any further demonstrations!

Angelo was in the drawing-room when she came downstairs. Golden eyes gleamed beneath dense ebony lashes, a faintly sardonic curve hardening his eloquent mouth as he returned her perusal. Her chest tightened. She felt as if she had gone down in a lift too fast. And the spacious room suddenly felt claustrophobic.

'What would you like to drink?' he drawled smoothly.

He handed her the glass of pure orange with an edged smile of amusement that made her fingernails bite into the palm of her free hand.

'You weren't drunk on anything but desire this afternoon but I salute your choice,' he murmured lazily. 'Alcohol dulls all sensations.'

Her nails inflicted purple crescents on her palm. Her teeth ground together. She lifted her fiery head high. 'Don't you think this farce has gone far enough?'

'Farce is comedy. I notice that you're not laughing.'

'Few people laugh at threats, grotesque or otherwise,' Kelda countered fiercely.

A maid came in to announce dinner. Kelda sank down rigid-backed in a heavily carved chair in the dining-room. As soon as the main course had been served, she thrust up her chin. 'I did nothing to be ashamed of six years ago! You have no right to threaten me and no excuse to keep me here!' she told him angrily.

'*Nothing*?' Angelo repeated drily.

'Nothing,' Kelda reiterated with conviction. 'And the way you treated me was absolutely unforgivable! When you came into the library that night, that boy was trying to rape me——'

Angelo quirked a satiric ebony brow. 'Still tossing that old chestnut on the fire? Really *cara*...if you're in search of an extenuating circumstance for what you did that night, can't you do better than cry rape? In the light of your hot-blooded nature, I find it excessively hard to believe that rape would have been necessary.'

Furious colour flooded her cheeks, highlighting the brilliance of her green eyes. 'I was switching out the lamps,' she persisted doggedly. 'I thought I was alone. He came up behind me and forced me down on to the floor. He hit me...' her voice trailed away, her facial muscles tightening as she forced herself to continue '...he b-bit my breasts and he hurt me...'

What shattered her was Angelo's raw burst of laughter. She had had to steel herself hard to describe that assault and she had been prepared to counter disbelief, but not the sheer earthy amusement raking through Angelo's lean, muscular frame.

'Love-bites,' he breathed in a sizzling undertone that somehow contrived to combine the lingering remnants of his amusement with complete disdain. 'I did notice them.'

'I am telling you the truth!' Kelda spat back at him tightly, painfully, outraged by his response. 'I was terrified...if you hadn't interrupted him, he would have got what he wanted!'

'You're not even a good liar,' Angelo whipped back with derision. 'The facts don't fit. You were in a dark room behind a firmly closed door. You didn't scream, you didn't demand that I call the police, nor did you come up with the attempted rape story until that boy was safely out of the house.'

Her stomach was churning with nausea. She could have explained all those things but why should she humiliate herself by persisting? Describing that assault even briefly had brought it alive again. The sensation of sick terror, overwhelming relief and shock had flooded back in a debilitating surge. Angelo's laughter and derision had been brutally inappropriate. Trying to defend herself was a waste of time.

Loathing was rippling through her in violent waves now. How dared he dismiss her story out of hand? How dared he talk as though she had been a promiscuous little slut at eighteen? The truth lay at the other extreme. Compared with her considerably more experienced friends, she had been almost laughably innocent. But what was that saying about one picture being worth a thousand words? Angelo had *seen* her in a compromising position and had chosen to see only what fitted his own interpretation of her character.

In the electric silence she stared down at the plate in front of her without appetite and with sudden decision, she stood up, emerald eyes flashing like polished gemstones in the pale, taut stillness of her face. 'I'm not hungry and I'm tired,' she said shortly.

'*Madre di Dio* . . .' Angelo breathed with driven impatience. 'You still sulk like a child!'

In the doorway, Kelda whirled round to face him again, all pale dignity banished by blazing anger. 'You hateful bastard . . . somehow, some day, I'll make you pay for bringing me here!'

As she strode through the hall, she paused beside an ornate marble and gilded side table. Angelo had tossed his car keys there earlier and they were still there, she noted with relief. She took the stairs two at a time, rage still storming through her veins in an energising tidal wave. Discarding the floral dress, she put on a pair of black leggings and a sweatshirt top before packing the remainder of her possessions. That small task taken care of, she sat down to wait for the rest of the household to go to bed.

It was one in the morning before Angelo retired for the night. She heard him passing by her room and froze for a second, but he didn't even hesitate at her door. To be safe, she waited for another forty minutes and then her heart thumping unnaturally loudly in her eardrums, she grabbed up her bag, opened her door as quietly as a mouse and crept downstairs. With her breath in her mouth, she slowly lifted his car keys off the side table before tip-toeing down to the room Angelo employed as an office.

She needed her passport and her money. No doubt she would eventually get home without the passport but it would be a lot easier if she could simply step right on to the first available flight. Afraid to turn on the desk lamp in case someone saw it shining out into the courtyard, she had to make do with the moonlight.

Her passport would be in his desk. It was the obvious place. She rummaged frantically through the drawers, only one of which was locked and that she left to the last. Biting her lip in frustration, she looked round for a suitable weapon to employ. She swooped on a paper knife and tried, nervous perspiration beading her brow, to force the lock. The knife scraped incredibly loudly across the wood when she failed.

It was an antique desk, built to last. She hacked with increasing desperation at the recalcitrant drawer, her nervous tension escalating by the minute. Finally, she acknowledged defeat. May you rot in hell, Angelo, she thought furiously. The window was not locked and it opened with the minimum of noise. She was halfway over the sill when she remembered the necklace.

With a curse, she wrenched at it and all but strangled herself! Using both hands, she attempted to pull it into breaking without lacerating her own throat. It was a considerably more difficult feat than she had imagined. Her neck bruised and sore, she gave up, and all the time her rage was building even higher. Hacking at Angelo's desk had made her feel like a criminal. She slid the rest of the way out the window and hurried across to the Porsche.

Angelo hadn't got all of her money. She had had some tucked for emergencies in her case. It would be sufficient to cover petrol if she needed any, at least one night's accommodation somewhere and telephone calls to arrange sufficient funds to travel home on. She would abandon the car in Pisa and head for the tourist office to ask what she had to do about her 'lost' passport.

Taking a deep breath, she started up the Porsche. It fired with a low growl and she filtered it slowly down towards the gates. Damn, they were shut! Leaping out, she opened them, dived back into the car and took off down the hill like a bullet.

Kelda was a confident driver but she had no map. She had driven quite a few miles before she came on a small town. There she slowed down in search of a signpost. A car came up close behind her and flashed its lights. Ignorant pig, she thought, so I'm not going fast enough! When a police siren went off, that same car overtook her at speed and pulled across the road in front of her, forcing her to a halt. She was thunderstruck.

She was arrested. The policeman spoke even less English than she spoke Italian but there were sufficient similarities between the languages for her to grasp with a sinking heart that she was being accused of stealing the car. Dear God, Angelo had reported the Porsche stolen! Her inability to produce her passport only exacerbated the situation.

Within half an hour, Kelda was in a police cell. It was a small town, an even smaller station and it was the middle of the night. Clearly there was nobody available to question her in English.

'*Domani* . . .' the policeman said in receipt of her shattered protests. Tomorrow. Tomorrow, it would be sorted out.

Kelda was in a blind panic by then. It had finally dawned on her that she *had* stolen Angelo's Porsche and that if he wanted to proceed with such a charge, he was probably well within his rights. She curled up on a bed with all the comfort of a funeral slab and burst into floods of tears. She was terrified. How was she going to explain what she had done?

It was dawn when the cell door was unlocked and she was taken into what appeared to be an interview room.

The policeman went out again and reappeared with Angelo.

Kelda took one paralysed look at him, flew out of her chair and threw herself at him. 'Angelo, get me out of here... please!' she sobbed.

He went rigid for a split second and then he closed his arms round her and said something in his own language to the policeman. Somebody else started talking. She took a deep shuddering breath and fought for self-control but she really was at the end of her tether.

Angelo guided her back out to the Porsche. 'How the hell could you be so stupid?' he raked at her as he pushed her into the passenger seat.

'How could you report your car stolen?' she gasped strickenly. '*How could you do that to me*?'

Angelo drove off at a mercilessly controlled speed. His profile was set like granite, tension emanating from him in waves. 'I did not report my car stolen. Stella saw it being driven off and got one of the maids to ring the police immediately. As it happens,' he shared with grating emphasis, 'they were already on their way. When you climbed out of the window of my study, you activated an alarm at the police station——'

'An alarm?' she echoed.

'A highly sophisticated security system installed to repel intruders,' Angelo spelt out fiercely. 'If it's activated and I don't call to say it was a mistake, naturally the police take it seriously. By the time I got out of bed, they were on the doorstep. When I saw the open window and the mess you've made of my desk, it did not instantly occur to me that *you* were the culprit——'

'Well, it should have done!' she raged at him with a sob tearing at her shaking voice.

'Do forgive me if I am not accustomed to a guest under my roof sneaking out of a window in the middle of the night and stealing my car!' Angelo flashed back at her with savage impatience.

'I was not stealing your car... I was b-borrowing it!' she blistered back hotly.

'You took my car without permission.'

'Oh, shut up about your bloody car!' Kelda shrieked at him. 'You took my passport and my money away! I was a prisoner! Of course I tried to escape... I'll never forgive you for what you've done to me tonight! Do you hear me?'

'*Sta zitto!*' Angelo bit out wrathfully.

'No, I will not keep quiet. Why sh-should I?' she sobbed furiously at him. 'I was locked up like a common criminal——'

'You were arrested because you were driving a car that had been reported stolen. It was a misunderstanding and you are fortunate that the police, who drove me here to pick you up, were willing to be so helpful. You could have been locked up for the rest of the night.'

'I hate you so much I could kill you,' Kelda threw at him bitterly. 'What did you tell the police?'

'That we had had a lovers' tiff,' Angelo drawled silkily as he filtered the car to a halt in the courtyard. 'What else? Italian men understand and appreciate women of volatile temperament.'

'I *hate* you,' she said again, unable to think of anything more vicious to say in the state she was in.

'*Say that just one more time,*' Angelo bit out in a sizzling undertone across the bonnet of the Porsche.

'And you'll what?' she shouted back with seething contempt as she strode into the house. 'I hate you... I hate you... I hate you!'

A powerful hand caught her wrist and yanked her round in the hall.

Her teeth grinding together, Kelda collided with incandescent golden eyes. It was like falling on an electric fence. 'Let go of me!' she hissed. 'Or, so help me, I'll scream the place down!'

'Go ahead,' Angelo invited, hauling her roughly up against him. 'Scream.'

Kelda was in the grip of such fury that she took full advantage of the invitation. In a passion, she threw her head back and screamed so loudly she hurt her throat and choked. She waited in the simmering silence. Nobody came running. Her lashes fluttered in bemusement.

Before she could part her lips again, Angelo literally grabbed her off her feet. One minute she was standing on solid ground, the next she was airborne and on the way up the stairs. 'Put me down!' she screeched.

He kicked her bedroom door wide, kicked it shut again and dropped her down on the bed. 'Angelo——'

'Shut up.' He came down on top of her in one lithe movement, pinning her flat with his superior weight. She was in the act of struggling to raise a punitive knee when he brought his mouth down hard on hers.

Still in a fury, she dug her hands like claws into his luxuriant hair and then the passion flooded her in a roaring tidal wave. It came out of nowhere, attacked and took her prisoner. A passion so instantaneous it wiped out everything that had gone before it. Electrified by the raw, devouring heat of his mouth, she was possessed by an excitement so intense that she felt dizzy and disorientated.

Her blood was drumming in her veins, her heart hammering like crazy. She was hot and cold all over and unable to keep still. He delved between her lips with his tongue and her thighs trembled. He kissed her until she was breathless and burning, not a single part of her body untouched by the sheer intensity of her arousal.

He hauled her sweatshirt off with more impatience than finesse, burying his mouth with a muttered imprecation in the sweet valley between her heaving breasts. He struggled out of his shirt. She heard fabric tear and reached instinctively up to bring him back to her again, lacing her arms round his neck, her fingers lacing into his hair in an ecstasy of excitement.

He muttered something in Italian. He sounded shaken, unlike himself. He came back to her again, the black curling hair on his chest abrasive against her taut nipples, thrusting his hands beneath her back to force her into even more intimate contact with his hard, muscular length. A choked sigh of satisfaction escaped her as he crushed her against him. She couldn't get close enough to him and evidently he couldn't get close enough to her.

He pressed his mouth to an achingly sensitive pulse at the base of her throat and sensation stormed through her. His hands found the proud swell of her breasts with surprisingly gentle hands and shaped and stroked, deliberately not touching the hardened peaks until her muscles clenched with frustration and she arched her back and helplessly invited him to that deeper intimacy.

And then, with a soft laugh, he captured a taut nipple and laved it with his tongue, teasing with his sharp white teeth before taking the unbearably tender bud into the moist cave of his mouth. It was a sweet torment that drove claws of raw need into her quivering body, and when he employed the same technique on her other breast she began to moan and tremble, utterly possessed by the power of sensation.

He ran the tip of his tongue down over her taut stomach and a rush of heat made her hips jerk. She wanted to drag his mouth back to hers. She wanted him everywhere at once because her whole body was beginning to scream with the hunger he had incited. He skimmed off the remainder of her clothing in one bold movement, rolling on to his side to devour her mouth in a series of rough, deep, drugging kisses while he dispensed with his own.

He came back to her naked. He was hot and damp and very male and she gasped at the power of her own pleasure in the feel of his body against hers. It was so different, so alien and yet, strangely, so gloriously right. Her fingers spread over the satin-smooth skin of his back and he jerked as if she had pulled a string. Moving without warning, he took her swollen mouth in a sudden explosion of renewed passion, holding her down, letting his hand travel over her silky, quivering stomach to the tangle of red curls at the apex of her thighs.

Nothing she had so far experienced prepared her for the wild excitement that overwhelmed her when he explored the moist petals of her femininity. His touch was so exquisitely pleasurable that she cried out. She was on a high of unbearable sensation, twisting, turning, entirely at the mercy of her own needs, but on another level she was highly attuned to the same build-up of excitement in Angelo.

His breathing was fractured, his heartbeat thumping a tattoo beneath her spread fingers. He moved with lithe determination, gripping her thighs and pulling her to him.

'I have waited so long for this, *cara*...' he muttered almost savagely.

A faint feathering of instinctive fear of the unknown momentarily gripped her as she felt the swollen hardness of his manhood against her. But it was shattered by the hunger he had unleashed inside her. That hunger, too long denied, sought only satisfaction at whatever the cost. Yet she was naïvely unprepared for the driving force with which he invaded her body with his own and the sharp pang of pain which momentarily clenched her muscles and made her bite into the soft underside of her lower lip.

Angelo stilled and stared down at her. In the dawn light she could focus on him with clarity. His lustrous golden eyes betrayed a brief glimmer of rare uncertainty and narrowed, suddenly raking her hectically flushed face. 'I'm hurting you,' he whispered, not quite steadily.

The pain had gone as quickly as it had come but her untried body had yet to adjust to that most intimate invasion. 'No.' The denial was jerky, swift.

'You're so small,' he breathed, sinking his hands beneath her slender hips, lithely shifting between her thighs with a stifled groan of pleasure and splintering control.

She felt possessed then, utterly and completely. He moved on her, slowly, deliberately until all she could focus on was the extraordinary response of her own body. All control was gone. The savage rhythm took a hold of her and she burned up in a heatwave of sensation, crying out at the moment of climax and subsiding into an aftermath of pleasure so intense she almost passed out. Angelo curved both arms round her so tightly she could scarcely breathe, and with a sleepy smile she fell blissfully asleep.

When she woke up, Angelo was making love to her again. The curtains were closed. She didn't know whether it was day or night. It didn't matter. She didn't want to think, only feel. Angelo allowed no time for thought, even less for conversation. It was as though there was nothing but the moment to be lived for. He was ruthless in his single-minded pursuit of pleasure.

'What time it it?' she whispered when she opened her eyes again, grudgingly reluctant to obey the rousing hand on her shoulder.

'After midnight.' Angelo was dressed and that struck her as extraordinary.

'Midnight when?' she muttered gruffly, removing her dazed eyes from him to conceal her consternation.

'Yesterday you were arrested,' he filled in obligingly, and settled a laden tray down on the wildly tossed bed.

They had slept and made love through an entire day. It didn't seem real. She couldn't believe it had happened. Her...and Angelo. A fight and an explosion of passion that had overruled every intelligent thought.

'Are you not hungry?'

He looked so cool. That inflamed her. She had to bite at her tongue to silence it before she impulsively spoke her mind. And what could she say? He was lounging on the end of her bed as though he belonged there. His strong jawline was no longer blue-shadowed. His hair was still damp from a shower. He was immaculately clad in an Armani sweater and black designer jeans. He took her breath away. Drop-dead gorgeous and deadly.

Self-preservation uppermost, she reached for the tray. Steak and a Caesar salad.

'It's the one meal I can make,' Angelo drawled with mocking self-deprecation.

'The only one you can be bothered to make, you mean,' she translated without hesitation, but inwardly astonished that he should have gone to that amount of effort for anyone other than himself.

'Why should I cook when I can afford to pay other people to do it?'

Why the blazes were they talking about the contents of her plate? It was impossible that Angelo could be feeling as awkward as she did. Angelo was no stranger to the intimacy of the bedroom. The morning after could hold no discomfiture for a male of his experience. But she refused to show her own desperately seesawing emotions. She chewed every piece of steak at least forty-seven times. As long as she was eating, he couldn't expect conversation, and all the while she was engaged in coping with the stark reality of the past twenty-four hours.

Why? Why Angelo? How could Angelo make her lose control to this extent when other men, even men she had liked and respected, left her cold? At eighteen, he had awakened her sensuality and she had buried that discovery deep. And whether she liked it or not there were ties between them that until now she had refused to recognise. From thirteen to seventeen, until that final year he'd spent abroad, Angelo had been the dominant male in her life. She knew Angelo on levels that she took for granted.

She had forgotten nothing in six years. She knew that he could not abide disorder or unpunctuality, she knew that he loved fast cars... and, discreetly, even faster women. She knew that he positively thrived on the pressure of wheeling and dealing on the international money-market. And she knew so many little things too.

His shirts were specially made for him in Hong Kong. She knew what size socks he wore because she had given him socks Christmas after Christmas in lurid colours she was well aware that he would never wear. She knew he had to shave twice a day. She knew he still kept the horse he had loved as a teenager in the ritziest stable in the block. She knew that he had perfect white teeth, had never had a filling but went a whiter shade of pale at the prospect of his six-monthly dental check-up...

And that knowledge made Angelo seem dangerously familiar. But they were only superficial things, she reminded herself painfully. Furthermore, her previous acquaintance with Angelo had been formed when she was a child and he had been an adult, who stood over her in a position of trust. Was it that awareness which had made it so difficult for her to believe that Angelo *would* actually hurt her? For, if that was true, if that was to be her excuse, she had never been more wrong about anything in her life.

Angelo skated a brown forefinger over the back of her hand. 'Are you usually this quiet?'

'Without eight full hours of rest and three regular meals...yes,' she dismissed and resisted the urge to jerk her hand out of reach.

Pride demanded that she protect herself. Angelo despised her and yet she had gone to bed with him. Not just once either. She had fallen off the bandwagon into an orgy which not the most self-deceiving argument could excuse. Her sexual infatuation had made a victim out of her but it didn't have to be that way...no, it didn't, she told herself fierily. She was no man's victim.

It had happened. Wishing it hadn't would change nothing. Angelo had not realised that he was her first lover and she was ferociously grateful for the fact. She could not have borne the humiliation of Angelo knowing that he had proved to be the one male the Iceberg found irresistible. Better that Angelo should think that he was no more special than any other man her name had been linked with... as it was, Angelo looked so *bloody* triumphant that her teeth ground together.

'I need a shower,' she said abruptly, and viewed him expectantly.

'With company,' Angelo attached smoothly, viewing her with brilliant dark eyes that devoured.

She lowered her lashes in shock. Every bone and muscle in her body ached. He was an insatiable lover but she had naturally assumed that he was currently at bay. He had actually woken her up and fed her to sustain her through another session of torrid sex. Her stomach quivered with nausea. 'Forget it,' she said tartly.

'I can't,' Angelo confided in a husky murmur. 'I let you sleep as long as I could but I can't forget that in a few hours we'll be on separate flights back to London.'

She had forgotten that. The reminder was timely and she embraced it with enormous relief. It was over. She could live with that. It was over and she could return home and, if not forget it had ever happened, at least forgive herself. Her sexual infatuation had been exorcised, she told herself. She had surrendered once to her basic instincts and now, she was effectively cured and free...

'And there we must necessarily practise greater discretion,' Angelo pointed out silkily but she could hear the cool menace of steel in the assurance. 'Your mother would be needlessly distressed by our affair.'

'We're not having an affair,' Kelda told him in a stifled undertone of distaste as she reached for her robe, thrust her arms into it and sprang off the bed.

Angelo closed a lean hand on her wrist before she could brush past him. 'Perhaps you'd like to tell me what we are having?'

'In the future... nothing,' she spelt out, emerald eyes colliding furiously with impassive gold. 'What we had? A one-night stand. A little tacky, a little foolish, but that's all.'

Beautifully shaped brown fingers moved caressingly on the tender skin above her wrist. 'I have never had a one-night stand in my life.'

'I find that very hard to credit!'

'I expect you would, *cara*,' Angelo held her fast when she attempted to coolly pull free, 'since tacky little foolish experiences undoubtedly litter your past,' he incised with succinct derision, watching the blossoming of pink highlight her exquisite face. 'But *I* do not intend to feature on such a list.'

Kelda was trembling with rage. She yanked her arm free. 'Sorry, *caro* . . . you're already on it,' she spelt out like a spitting cat.

'Are you scared?' Angelo drawled lethally. 'Are you scared of the response you give me?'

She could still feel his fingerprints on her skin. Her mouth felt swollen, her breasts tender, her body almost frighteningly alien to her. And she looked at him and her chest went tight. Angelo emanated power in a force-field of energy. He was one hundred per cent in control. Nothing she had yet said had even angered him.

'Why should I be?' She blessed the mask of indifference she had learnt to assume on demand for the camera, for deep down inside she was sick and squirming at the necessity of the hard-bitten act he was forcing her to assume. 'Did you think you were somehow different from the others, Angelo? Do you think I gave you something more than I gave them? That's your ego talking,' she asserted with a scornful little smile on her wide, generous mouth. 'You're good . . . but you're not so good that I want to repeat the experience.'

He had gone white beneath his naturally dark complexion. Hooded eyes of black ice surveyed her and every nerve-cell in her quivering body tensed. Raw threat had tasted the atmosphere. Every scrap of playfulness had been wiped from his clenched, hard features. She could feel the violence in him. Inches below the civilised veneer dwelt the naked predator as wild as any animal, and she had always known that, known that Angelo's savage self-discipline and seething intelligence alone controlled that side of his temperament.

She had called up the devil in him, but he had given her no choice. Better to deal with Angelo as the hostile enemy she knew best than as the passionate lover he had proved to be. *That* Angelo she did not feel equipped to deal with. She stood her ground, hanging on to her faintly amused smile with rigorous determination. It was over now. He would leave her alone. Angelo, chased by her sex practically from the edge of the cradle, would not continue his pursuit in receipt of such a scathing rejection.

'Have you anything else to add?' His wine-dark voice trickled like the gypsy's curse down her taut spinal cord.

'Angelo,' she sighed, shrugging a shoulder, 'you *know* what I'm like. I like variety——'

'You're a whore,' he breathed in a raking undertone of suppressed and seething rage. 'You disgust me.'

Disturbingly, the brutal admission stabbed like a knife into her. A sudden haze of moisture interrupted her vision of him, brightening her green eyes to luminescence. But she stared him down, only dimly registering that she was shaking all over, her legs like cotton wool supports.

'And to think that you excited me so much that I took no precautions,' Angelo drawled between gritted teeth, shooting her a look of such savage loathing that she was pinned there like a butterfly to a specimen board. 'I hope I do not live to regret the omission.'

As the door slammed on his exit, Kelda stared at the space where he had been with stunned eyes and parted lips. He had said...he had said he had not used contraception and he was afraid that *he* might live to regret it! Kelda was ingloriously sick in the bathroom, her body's response to the horrendous scene she had forced. Only then did the tears come, slow and painful as thorns being plucked from her flesh, and what was worst was that she really didn't know why she was crying.

CHAPTER SIX

'WE'RE dining with Tomaso and Daisy this evening...'

Kelda threw her head up from the English newspaper she had been doggedly studying. Her fiery mane of curls flew in all directions. 'I beg your pardon?'

Angelo dealt her a look of black-ice warning. 'I said that I would bring you with me——'

'An ambitious guy, aren't you?' Kelda snaked back at him, her eyes awash with disbelief behind the screen of her dark glasses. She had had to force herself to come down and join him for breakfast. He would have read a request for a tray in her room as weakness. Since she had been unforgivably weak in other departments, she could not fall short of her own expectations yet again. For that reason, she was seated here in the courtyard, struggling to swallow food that threatened to choke her and make no pointless comment concerning the passport and wallet which she had discovered by her plate.

'I have no intention of permitting the conflict between us to damage their relationship——'

'And when was this cosy little arrangement made?' Kelda breathed shakily.

'Before you left London. Your mother said that you wouldn't come——'

'She was right!'

'I said that you would...and you will,' Angelo swore with an emphasis that was disturbingly chilling. 'We will arrive together and we will leave together. We will be polite and pleasant to each other in their company——'

'*Bloody hell*!' Kelda gasped inelegantly, too disconcerted by this unlikely vision to conceal her reaction.

'Polite and pleasant,' Angelo repeated drily. 'Your mother's fears will then be put to rest. Your feelings will cease to be a matter of concern to her——'

'I'm not playing happy families for your benefit!' Kelda bit out.

Dear lord, she was thinking sickly, he had planned the evening even before she'd arrived in Italy. He had promised her mother what must have seemed the impossible and he had never doubted that he could deliver. Her blood ran cold.

'Your life will be a living hell if you don't, I promise you that.'

The husky deepening of his rich vowel sounds made the hair prickle at the nape of her neck. Accidentally she clashed with hard dark eyes, bottomless as a well shaft to the unwary. Her sensitive stomach turned over. She bent her head. She would have gone, no matter what he did or said. But Angelo would never believe that. He seemed to think that she had a malicious need to damage their parents' relationship.

Yet without even realising it, she had come to terms with that renewed bond. Once again, Daisy had unfairly dropped the news on her without any prior warning of what was to come. It had been rather like a ghastly re-run of the bridal couple's visit to her school all those years ago. And Kelda was uncomfortably aware that she had reacted with no more maturity this time than she had then.

But once the shock of Daisy's announcement had worn off, Kelda had accepted that her response had been entirely selfish. She had upset her mother. She had focused, not on her mother's potential happiness, but on her own determination not to be forced into contact with Angelo again. That admitted, however, Angelo had merely exacerbated the situation by launching straight into attack that night at her apartment. After all, she reflected bitterly, Angelo had had three months, not twenty-four hours to adjust to their parents' reconciliation.

'Is that understood?' Angelo probed.

She bit her tongue and tasted blood. It tasted of defeat. 'Yes!' she slung the word at him. 'But your interference was unnecessary.'

'The car will be here to pick us up in half an hour.'

Her throat closing over, she took the dismissal with head held high, but she seethed with such a turmoil of emotion that she marvelled she didn't just explode. Messily, loudly, stupidly. Perhaps, at last, she was learning. Impulse and temper, her two biggest failings, invariably got her into trouble around Angelo. Angelo rejoiced in being neither impulsive nor uncontrolled, and that, she registered painfully, was why Angelo was in the ascendant.

When would she start feeling better? *When*? Because right now . . . right now, she felt worse than she had last night and that was saying something! She had not slept. She had paced the floor. She had cried. Coming to philosophical terms with the fact that she had gone to bed with Angelo was proving far more difficult than she had hoped. His powerful sexuality had been her downfall. She wasn't the only woman to make such a mistake in the heat of passion . . . and she wouldn't be the last. But for how long was she to feel guilty, ashamed, miserable? And why should she feel soiled by the promiscuous pretence she had put on for his benefit?

Hadn't she only given him what he expected? Angelo despised her. But that hadn't prevented him from using her in the most vicious way of all. Her own wanton sensuality had been his weapon of destruction. She would not allow him to wield that weapon ever again. It was finished, over. One day of insanity. It had taught her a hard lesson. Surely there would be no further complications?

It wasn't that easy to get pregnant . . . was it? She was not some silly teenager . . . but she had acted as recklessly as one. Angelo had clearly assumed that she was on the contraceptive pill. Angelo, she thought hysterically, had been more concerned at the threat of having caught some dread disease. From a virgin. And he hadn't noticed. She had once read that men often couldn't tell the difference.

She never spoke a word the whole way to the airport in the limousine. Like a stretcher case, she was in limbo. But she could literally *feel* Angelo's presence. The atmosphere vibrated round Angelo. Always. Utterly different from his father, he had volcanic energy and equally volcanic moods. But here in Italy she had seen a side of Angelo that she had never known existed.

Angelo, flirtatious, teasing, infuriating. Angelo, passionate, irresistible, even sympathetic. As a teenager, she had not understood that, below the surface ice, Angelo absolutely seethed and burned with emotion. Then he had seemed merely grim, forbidding and sarcastic. Now, she was painfully conscious of the scorching atmospheric undertones.

'I'll pick you up at seven tonight,' he drawled.

Climbing out, she simply ignored him.

'Kelda . . . ?'

As she waited for the chauffeur to extract her case, a hand like an iron vice suddenly hooked on to her shoulder. Before she could react, she was flattened up against the side of the limousine with Angelo's hard, muscular body plastered to hes. He took her mouth in an unrestrained demonstration of sexual aggression. But she still caught fire and burned. Aware of every lithe line of his powerful body, she could feel the force of his own arousal, and that made her knees buckle.

She felt his fingers brush the back of her neck and she didn't realise what he was doing until he stepped back with the necklace in his hand. She blinked in bemusement. She had actually forgotten that she was still wearing it. He dropped the glittering emeralds into her palm and closed her unsteady fingers round them.

'Seven,' he said again. 'Or would you like me to come earlier?'

She scraped herself almost clumsily off the car, all the while helplessly hypnotised by the scorching hunger, blatantly burnishing his golden eyes. That hunger pulled hot strings inside her. Oxygen snarled up in her convulsed throat. It was the excitement that frightened her the most. The most incredible, explosive excitement that thrummed and throbbed between them in waves of heat.

'*Dio*,' Angelo sighed in a tigerish growl of dissatisfaction. 'I have a meeting at four.'

'I disgust you,' Kelda reminded him shakily.

'When I'm out of bed. In it, you drive me crazy,' Angelo dropped in a sizzling purr and swinging on his heel, he walked away.

Unnoticed by either of them, a photographer, standing on the far side of the car park, lowered his camera with a satisfied smile.

On her commercial flight, she thought of his far more comfortable journey in his private jet. Like a married man with a mistress, he was covering their tracks. But she had no intention of becoming Angelo's mistress and it was a shock to appreciate that her little performance the night before had not killed that ambition of his stonedead. That utterly ridiculous ambition. If he hadn't taken her so much by surprise in that car park, she would have pushed him away, she told herself.

There was a promising call on her answering machine from the estate agent when she got back. A cash offer for her apartment and more than she had expected to receive. When she went straight back out again to see the agent, she was even more pleased to hear that the buyer was interested in purchasing most of her furniture as well. She would be moving to a rented apartment and she didn't want the cost of storage.

'There shouldn't be any problem,' the agent extolled cheerfully. 'He's a Swiss executive, buying on behalf of his company, and fortunately for you he particularly liked the location of your apartment. They want possession by the end of the month. Get round to your solicitor and sign on the dotted line as soon as possible ... before the guy realises that he could have got a better deal elsewhere.'

She went straight away and it cost her a pang or two of regret. Owning her own apartment had symbolised success. Selling it underlined how much Danny Philips' lies had cost her. But she was sensible enough to acknowledge that she had aimed rather too high when she had bought, and that if ever she was in the same position again she would be much more modest in her requirements.

The bell went about six when she was in the shower. It was Russ Seadon, the photographer whose talents had first catapulted her to fame. He was engaged to Gina Delfont, another model, who was also Kelda's closest friend. She often stayed with them when she was working in New York and was happy to return their hospitality whenever she could.

Russ dropped his bag in her guest-room and spent half an hour catching up on all the news before settling down with a pizza in front of the television. Kelda paced her bedroom floor, dreading the evening ahead. Angelo wasn't going to leave her alone. He wasn't going to make things that easy for her.

And she was out of her depth with Angelo. When he touched her, intelligence went out of the window, and if anything more happened between them she would never forgive herself. He wanted to use her for sexual release alone. Her skin crawled at the awareness of how vulnerable she had become. Somehow Angelo had to be *made* to walk back out of her life again ... but how? What would most anger Angelo?

Absently she winced at the clatter Russ was making in her kitchen and then her furrowed brow cleared. The belief that she had another man in her life would most anger Angelo...and here she was with another man staying under her very roof...

'You want me to what?' Russ echoed dazedly ten minutes later.

Kelda's cheeks were hot with growing embarrassment. 'Forget it!' she urged hurriedly. 'It was a stupid idea——'

Suddenly, Russ laughed. 'This guy won't take no for an answer...is that it?'

Kelda nodded. 'All I want you to do is look at home here, as if you're waiting up for me,' she spelt out awkwardly.

'He's not likely to get violent, is he?' Russ checked.

She shook her head and prayed that she was right.

Russ grinned on his way out of the door with her spare key. 'Don't worry, I'll be back in time. I think I'm going to enjoy this!'

Kelda got dressed, selecting a clinging trouser-suit in shocking pink. It had strategic and daring cut-outs and she wore it like a suit of armour, calculated to repel. Angelo's dainty little blonde women were invariably given to conservative wardrobes.

'You look like a trapeze artist. It suits you.' Infuriatingly, Angelo let his lustrous dark eyes travel over her with offensive and blazingly confident familiarity.

Kelda tossed the emerald necklace carelessly into the glove compartment of his Ferrari.

'Is that some sort of a statement?' Angelo drawled, lazily unconcerned by the gesture.

'I don't want it.'

'It belongs to you now. I gave it to you.'

Her breath quickened, her pulse-rate accelerating as her tension increased. 'But I don't want anything from you,' she stressed, striving to keep her voice level and cool.

'Perhaps this is not a good time to tell you that I am in the process of buying your apartment.'

Her head whipped round in shock. 'Too late. You've missed the boat!' she returned sharply. 'I agreed the sale today.'

'With whom?'

'A Swiss company.'

'I own the company.'

The soft assertion dragged a soft sound of incredulity from her throat. Wide-eyed, she stared at him. '*You* own it?'

'Who else would pay over the odds to secure your ownership?' Angelo queried drily. 'I'll sign it back to you as soon as the sale is complete——'

'Why would you want to buy my apartment for me?' Kelda demanded, anger and a kind of threatened horror coalescing out of her shock.

'I told you in Italy that I would pick up all the bills,' Angelo reminded her smoothly. 'And naturally that includes securing your home for your occupancy. I'll sort out all your financial problems. I will clear your credit cards, settle any outstanding debts and make arrangements for an allowance to be paid into your account.'

In a daze, she listened while he listed his intentions. A dark mist of humiliation enveloped her. Her fair skin reddened in a painful flush. And then anger stirred out of her disbelief. 'I'm not a fixture you can buy along with my apartment!' she asserted rawly. 'I am not for sale!'

'I didn't say that you were,' Angelo murmured with calm emphasis. 'But we made an agreement in Italy——'

'There was no agreement!' Kelda blitzed back at him.

'Shall we say that when you allowed me access to that exquisite body I rather took agreement for granted.'

The flush drained away, leaving her pale. She wanted very badly to claw at him for his ruthless determination to portray her as greedy, immoral and sexually available. She had never hated him as much as she did in that moment, could not comprehend how that hatred had failed to kill all desire for him . . . yet, it had failed quite spectacularly. All of a sudden, she was very grateful that if Angelo came back to her apartment tonight he would be greeted by Russ. Even Angelo would not be able to disregard so blatant a rejection!

Even so, she found that she was still trembling with the sheer force of her emotions. 'I told you that it was over in Italy . . . I made that crystal-clear,' she told him tightly, staring rigidly out of the windscreen. 'It was a mistake I don't intend to repeat and I never at any stage had any intention of becoming your mistress. So you've just bought yourself an empty apartment, Angelo. I will be moving out within the month.'

'I don't think so,' Angelo murmured silkily and parked the car.

She walked ahead of him into the restaurant, quickly espying her mother's blonde head in a corner. Daisy was openly relieved at their arrival, Tomaso rising with alacrity to at first advance his hand and then smilingly give her a light kiss on the cheek. He was thinner and older-looking than she remembered and her eyes pricked with unexpected tears as she registered the extent of the happiness glowing in her mother's face.

'A bit of a coincidence, you both being in Italy at the same time,' Tomaso observed heartily, ordering up a round of aperitifs.

'Were you——?' Kelda turned to Angelo with manufactured surprise.

'You wouldn't have run into each other,' Tomaso assured her. 'Angelo was in the south, inspecting a factory . . . isn't that right?' he added, addressing his son.

'How terribly boring,' Kelda sighed with mock sympathy, encountering a chilling black glance of warning from beneath Angelo's long, luxuriant lashes. A slight darkening over his hard cheekbones told her that he was not wholly at ease lying to his trusting *papa*. She was bitterly amused by the discovery.

In other circumstances, it might have been a pleasant evening. Tomaso was on tremendously good form. He kept on patting her mother's arm possessively, stealing little glances at her and smiling. It was clear that he too was very happy. The wedding was discussed. A date was already in the offing which suggested that Angelo's belief that she had the power to prevent their remarriage by influencing her mother had been grossly exaggerated.

'You really don't mind?' Daisy prompted in the cloakroom.

Kelda embraced her much smaller mother and murmured, 'If Tomaso makes you happy, I'm happy.'

'Good...so what's going on between you and Angelo?' Daisy enquired anxiously.

Kelda froze. 'Going on?'

'Don't treat me as if I'm stupid or blind,' Daisy breathed ruefully. 'I'm neither. A week ago, you were furious at the idea of Tomaso's and my getting back together again——'

'I was being childish and selfish——'

'When Angelo told me that he would bring you here tonight to dine with us, I told him he was aiming at the moon,' her mother shared. 'But here you are just like he promised and he keeps on watching you and you keep on touching him——'

'Touching him?' Kelda echoed blankly.

'A couple of times, you've put your hand on his arm when you've been speaking——'

'Really?' Kelda said weakly because she couldn't remember doing it.

'And I know you,' her mother persisted. 'You're not the sort of a person who touches others unless you're very familiar with them, and Angelo of all people——'

'Mum, don't you think you're——?'

'And why is he looking at you all the time?' Daisy demanded worriedly. 'And you never looked at him once——'

'Maybe I'm just not that comfortable with Angelo,' Kelda suggested unsteadily, shaken by her mother's unexpected perception.

'He is very, very good-looking,' Daisy remarked uneasily. 'And very clever. He has a lot of charm when he wants to use it——'

'You sound as if you don't like him very much——'

'I don't want you to be hurt again,' her mother whispered. 'Angelo isn't the settling down type and there's something different about you, Kelda...'

Dear heaven, the mother with X-ray vision! Concealing her panic at Daisy's persistence, Kelda forced a smile. 'Being pleasant to Angelo takes a lot out of me.'

After the interrogation about a couple of gestures she hadn't even been aware of making, it was a relief when the evening came to an end. Angelo slid silently into the Ferrari.

'Thank goodness that's over,' Kelda muttered, massaging her temples which were starting to ache with the onset of a tension headache.

'What did you tell Daisy?' Angelo shot at her without warning.

'Nothing! And you can stop treating me like your partner in crime,' Kelda told him flatly, bitterly. 'I am not in the habit of lying to my mother and I didn't enjoy doing it.'

'You told her something,' Angelo repeated darkly.

'One more word and I'm calling a cab!' Kelda swore. 'If I'd told her anything, she would have been so shattered, the entire restaurant would have known about it before we got out!'

'It won't matter once they're married. They'll spend most of their time abroad. It will seem natural that I should visit my stepsister——'

'Angelo... I want nothing to do with you!' she practically screamed at him in frustration. 'Why do you find that so impossible to accept?'

He insisted on seeing her right to the door of her apartment. He was walking right into the trap without the smallest encouragement from her. Her headache had turned into a killer by the time he took her key from her and unlocked the door. Russ would be waiting...she hoped. Then it would all be at an end.

'You're not feeling well.' Angelo pressed her over the threshold and followed her in. 'Can I get you anything?'

That he had noticed surprised her. 'I'll be fine.' Her exasperated gaze was probing the lounge for Russ. He wasn't there.

'Will you be all right?' Abruptly Angelo swore and stilled, the hand at her spine dropping away.

Kelda's strained green eyes widened to their fullest extent as Russ strolled out of her bedroom, only a small towel wrapped round his hips. 'I thought you were never coming home, darling,' he sighed reproachfully, and smiled at Angelo. 'Thanks for bringing her back safely.'

Outraged incredulity had clenched Angelo's hard dark features. He swung round. 'You bitch,' he grated in a shaken undertone, seemingly unable to take his eyes off Russ.

Kelda was trembling. The look in Angelo's eyes was flat and cold and dead. And somehow that terrified her. She had to resist an extraordinary and utterly ridiculous urge to start explaining that Russ was a close friend of the platonic variety, pretending to be something else at her request.

'I couldn't believe...' Angelo fell silent, shot her a glance of such smouldering violence that she stumbled back against the wall, afraid of physical attack. The front door thudded shut in his wake. Kelda sagged like a rag doll.

Russ sighed. 'How did I do?'

'You were incredible.' Her own voice sounded as if it was coming from miles away. Her head felt as if it was about to split wide open.

'You weren't having second thoughts about me doing this, were you?' Russ studied her shuttered white face anxiously.

'Of course not.'

It was done. It was over. Angelo was gone . . . but why did that knowledge hurt so much?

Russ expelled his breath. 'I thought it would be funny, but it wasn't,' he acknowledged. 'Rossetti was shattered.'

'His ego was dented . . . that's all,' Kelda mumbled, suddenly deathly tired and drained.

Kelda's week in New York modelling designer knitwear stretched to five weeks in the end. Russ had tugged some useful strings, put her on the cover of two glossy magazines and all of a sudden she had found that her career was taking off again. For a month she was heavily in demand. Ella was constantly on the phone to her and slowly but surely she got word of possible assignments back home as well. The world had a short memory. Danny Philips was old news.

She was flicking through her diary on the flight back to London when she noticed. She raked through the pages again, certain she had made a mistake. But she had not made an oversight. There was no familiar little cross marking the start of her last period. She was three weeks overdue.

She sat there in a blank haze of shock, suddenly cold and shivery. Her heart had plunged to her stomach and her stomach felt as if she had swallowed an indigestible lump of concrete. It had felt like that several times before over the past ten days. She had lost weight through her lack of appetite but that hadn't worried her. A model could never be too thin for the camera.

She had blocked out those days in Italy very efficiently since leaving London. Work had been her panacea, her saviour. She had been too busy and too tired to torment herself with vain regrets for what couldn't be altered. It was over. She had made a mistake.

She could learn to live with that... that was what she had told herself when her mind strayed.

And now this. It couldn't happen to her, she had thought in Italy, brushing that spur of fear away with confidence. She had never thought about being pregnant, couldn't even imagine being pregnant, and now she was faced with the possibility that she might well be. In defiance, she listed all the other things that might have made her late, but the cloud of dark foreboding refused to lift.

She bought a pregnancy test at the airport. Even that embarrassed the hell out of her. Her name came over the public address system while it was being wrapped and she froze.

Tomaso and Daisy had come to meet her off the plane but traffic had held them up. She was touched, but her recent purchase weighed like lead in her holdall.

'We've got a surprise for you,' Daisy asserted.

Kelda gave her mother a rather weak smile and climbed into the back of Tomaso's stately Rolls. 'What sort of a surprise?'

'The cottage is yours,' her mother pointed out. 'And after next week I won't be needing it any more——'

Next week—the wedding that Kelda was dreading.

'Tomaso wanted to buy your apartment but it went very quickly, didn't it?' Daisy sighed. 'I assumed it would be on the market for ages and I was wrong——'

Kelda bent her head, not knowing where to look. She had found a rented flat in Highgate before she went to New York and her mother had promised to supervise the removal of her personal possessions when Kelda had discovered that she wouldn't be back in London in time to make the move herself.

'I want you to have the cottage back. After all, you bought it for me,' Daisy stressed.

'A very generous gesture on your income.' Tomaso dealt her a warm approving smile. 'I will always be grateful that you looked after your mother when she wouldn't allow me to look after her.'

'I don't need anybody looking after me,' Daisy muttered a shade tartly, but she beamed at Tomaso all the same.

The cottage. Kelda hadn't even thought about it. But she was driven back there. Her own cushions adorned her mother's chairs. And Daisy's display of ruby glass in the lounge had been displaced by the ornamental frogs Kelda had been collecting since childhood. Her mother squeezed her elbow. Kelda blinked back tears.

The cottage had two dormer bedrooms, both with en-suite facilities, a lounge and a cosy dining-room open on to the kitchen as well as a small but very private garden. All of a sudden she had a home of her own again. She sat down on the edge of the bed and then tore into her holdall for the test.

'What do you want for dinner?' Daisy called upstairs brightly.

'I'm not hungry!'

'Rubbish!'

Forty minutes later she knew, but she sat on the side of the bath simply staring at the kit, telling herself that maybe she had done the test wrong and re-reading the instructions. She felt terribly sick and even more terribly scared. She felt just like a teenager, not like an adult at all. Pregnant. It was a black joke. She couldn't believe she was, couldn't credit that one mistake could lead to such frightening consequences.

Three days later, her mother found her being sick in the bathroom for the second morning in succession. 'You've caught some bug,' Daisy muttered anxiously. 'This time, I'm not listening to you, I'm calling the doctor!'

'No!'

Ignoring her protests, her mother marched over to the phone.

Kelda was already under sufficient stress '*Don't!*'

'Don't be silly.' Daisy continued to dial.

'For goodness' sake, I'm not sick...I'm pregnant!' Kelda suddenly sobbed in frustration and then a silence, utterly unlike any other, fell as Daisy stared back at her in disbelief and Kelda realised what she had said. She had not intended to tell her mother until she returned from her honeymoon.

It took an hour to calm Daisy down.

Her own eyes as swollen as her parent's, Kelda whispered, 'I didn't want you to know yet.'

'How am I going to tell Tomaso?'

'Don't you dare tell Tomaso!' Kelda gasped.

'He's going to have to know some time! Kelda...how could you go to bed with some man you hardly know at a party?' Her mother broke down in tears again.

That seemed the worst aspect of it all in her parent's eyes. Kelda turned her head away, wishing that she could have told the truth but in the circumstances that was impossible. She didn't sleep a wink that night. Tomorrow, Daisy and Tomaso were getting married. And she had ruined her mother's wedding for her with the sort of news few parents wished to hear. Her conscience was in agony. And as if that wasn't enough, she knew that tomorrow she would have to face Angelo again.

Would she tell him? How *could* she tell him? The right words for such an announcement evaded her. After he had seen Russ strolling out of her bedroom half naked, why should he even believe that her baby was *his*? Too exhausted to even think any more, Kelda lay there in the darkness, wrapped in turmoil.

When she came down for breakfast, Daisy was astonishingly all smiles and buoyance. 'You could get a nanny and we could keep the baby when you had to be away overnight. Tomaso loves children. He'll probably be delighted when he gets over the...the surprise,' Daisy selected tactfully. 'After all, society has changed. Single parenthood is much more acceptable these days. Would you like one rasher or two?'

'Mum, I——' Kelda hesitated and then abruptly found herself wrapped in her mother's arms. 'The smell of that bacon makes me sick,' she confided with a tiny catch in her voice.

The wedding was at a register office. The first person Kelda saw was Angelo, and the effect of Angelo sheathed in a superb light grey suit was powerful. She stumbled in the doorway, briefly unable to take her eyes off him. Dear lord, the ground beneath her feet seemed to tilt and her skin was damp and her heart was racing. Eyes of gold deep enough to drown in, ebony hair that felt like silk against her fingertips. A welter of erotic imagery she had locked tight within her memory banks suddenly overwhelmed her.

'That's Fiona,' her mother hissed. 'I forgot to mention that she'd be coming. Gorgeous, isn't she? Tomaso thinks she's been the most promising yet. She's a banker and she has two degrees——'

'Two degrees,' Kelda muttered jerkily, her stomach a rolling turmoil of nausea as she belatedly focused on the six-foot-plus-tall Amazon standing beside Angelo. From her waterfall-straight black hair and bright sapphire-blue eyes to the soles of her elegantly shod feet, Fiona was stunning.

'I was so silly that night we all dined together,' Daisy whispered in haste as Tomaso bore down on them. 'I had this stupid idea that Angelo and you were——'

Tomaso's arrival mercifully silenced her mother.

He has another woman. Well, what did you expect…why are you so shocked? Kelda couldn't answer that question. She knew only that the sight of Angelo with another woman had devastated her. The brief ceremony over, she swiftly spun on her heel and approached Tomaso's brother and his wife. 'Would you mind giving me a lift back to the——?'

'You can come with us, Kelda.' Angelo's husky voice was like a knife between her ribs.

Slowly she turned round. Angelo smoothly introduced Fiona. Fiona gave her a muted smile, her bright eyes sharply assessing. 'I've heard so much about you that I feel I know you already.'

'Bad news does tend to travel fast.'

'Kelda,' Angelo breathed with icy emphasis.

Treating him to the first look she had dared, she clashed with impassive dark eyes and felt the ice there like a chilly hand squeezing her heart.

'She's what?' she heard Tomaso roar very loudly several feet away.

'I didn't mean to offend you,' Fiona was saying drily. 'But I'm sorry if I did.'

'No, I'm sorry.' Kelda breathed in deeply, struggling to maintain her mask of composure. 'I'm a bit touchy today.'

'Do you want a lift?' Angelo enquired uninvitingly.

A hand came down on her shoulder. 'Kelda will drive back to the house with us,' Tomaso announced grim-mouthed. 'We have something very personal to discuss, Angelo.'

CHAPTER SEVEN

WHITE and strained, Kelda couldn't resist throwing a reproachful glance at her mother. 'You didn't waste any time, did you?'

'Naturally your mother confided in me,' Tomaso responded thinly. 'I am her husband and your stepfather. Is it true? Are you expecting a child?'

'Mum, how could you do this to me?' Kelda muttered in deep embarrassment.

'We're going off on our honeymoon and I don't like leaving you alone,' Daisy told her ruefully. 'I needed Tomaso's advice.'

'You always were...volatile,' Tomaso muttered half under his breath.

'It's none of your business!' Kelda burst out helplessly. She wasn't a child.

'But is it Angelo's business?' Tomaso's sharp dark eyes rested astutely on her startled face.

'What's this got to do with Angelo?' Daisy demanded blankly.

Tomaso had removed his wallet from an inside pocket. Opening it, he extracted a piece of folded newspaper. 'Don't you think Angelo would be preferable to some stranger at a party?' he said drily, and handed the cutting to his new bride.

'What's that?' Kelda demanded in a high, thin voice that was shredding fast into near hysteria.

'Where and when was this photo taken?' Daisy had paled in shock. She looked at her daughter with appalled eyes. 'Why didn't you tell me? I'm your mother.'

'It was taken at Pisa almost six weeks ago. That's the airport in the background. It was published in a minor gossip mag in Italy and someone sent it to me. I've had it for weeks,' her stepfather admitted with a small tight smile. 'I didn't want to upset you, *cara*.'

Kelda snatched at the cutting and turned a deep guilty-as-charged pink. It was a photo of them kissing at the airport and Angelo was very recognisable even if only a tutored eye might have guessed *her* identity.

'They were in Italy together,' Tomaso breathed harshly.

'You mean that they both pretended ... they *lied*?' her mother gathered in horror. 'But why?'

'Since your daughter appears to have lost her voice, I'm depending on my son to fill in the blanks——'

'No, please!' Kelda broke in. 'It isn't Angelo's ... I mean, definitely not ... I just can't imagine Angelo and I together *that* way——' Literally stupefied by the horror of Tomaso's discovery that she had been in Italy with Angelo, Kelda was having a very hard time finding convincing words of denial.

Her stepfather dealt her an intuitive look. 'Can't you?' he fielded even more drily. 'You were alone with Angelo for what ... three days? I wouldn't trust the two of you to be alone together for an hour——'

'Tomaso!' Daisy gasped in reproof.

'My son has wanted your daughter practically from the first moment he laid eyes on her, and judging by a certain episode six years ago Kelda was not——'

'It is not Angelo's child!' Kelda suddenly sobbed, covering her face.

'Then you have nothing to worry about when I tell him,' Tomaso told her speciously.

Kelda reeled out of the limousine outside the mansion she had spent five years of her life in. She surged through the wide open front door, deaf and blind to the housekeeper's greeting and dived into the downstairs cloakroom at the back of the huge hall. She lost her breakfast there.

When she made a strained reappearance, everyone was being seated in the ballroom which had been set out with tables for the reception. It was milling with guests and caterers and she had never been so grateful to see crowds. She was less grateful when she found herself at the top table, only several seats down from Angelo and Fiona.

The meal and the speeches were ever afterwards a blur. Tomaso had shattered her. Never before had she been made so aware of the likeness between father and son. Her stepfather had not previously shown that side of his temperament to her. There was dancing after the meal. She wanted to go home, but knew that she had to sit it out. Several men asked her to dance and grimly, for the sake of appearances, she obliged. She averted her eyes every time she caught a glimpse of Angelo and Fiona on the floor, didn't even question why she had to protect herself that way.

When Angelo smoothly cut in on her partner as the music changed, she was quite unprepared for the confrontation. Instinctively, she stilled and the lean hand at her spine pulled her closer. 'Smile,' he suggested silkily, raking dark eyes absorbing the sudden tense pallor freezing her beautiful face. 'Or I might suspect that you're pining for me.'

Her nostrils flared on the disturbingly familiar scent of him. Her fluid body was poker straight in the circle of his arms. 'I don't smile for you, Angelo,' she said.

'Except in my bed,' he murmured with black velvet satire.

Involuntarily, Kelda flinched and missed a step.

'Yes...you are rather sensitive today,' he mused softly into the veiling torrent of her hair and her skin tightened painfully over her bones as his breath warmed her throat. 'And you lack your usual glow——'

'Still stuck with my apartment?' Kelda interjected tautly. 'I hope you make a loss on it.'

'Sold at profit to an impatient Arab,' Angelo drawled. 'Though a loss wouldn't have bothered me. I had what I wanted, after all...and should I ever want it again,

I'm convinced I wouldn't be disappointed. You don't play hard to get by any stretch of the imagination——'

White as death, Kelda pulled free just as the music stopped. 'You bastard,' she whispered tightly and headed back to her seat, savaged by his cruelty.

Her mother dropped down into the empty chair beside her and said, 'Tomaso has calmed down.'

'Good…I'm sorry,' Kelda sighed. 'I've wrecked your day.'

'That's nonsense. I've never been so happy,' Daisy carolled a little tipsily. 'And if it's Angelo's baby, that makes it OK, doesn't it? Tomaso says, he'll have to marry you and so he should, seducing my little girl——'

'I am not a little girl, Mother!' Kelda hissed, aghast.

'You are measured up against Angelo. Tomaso says it serves him right…'

'It isn't Angelo's ba——'

Daisy frowned at her. 'Don't lie to me any more, Kelda. I deserve better than that.'

'I'm sorry.'

'I forgive you. It's your hormones. They make you moody.' With a dizzy smile, her mother drifted off again.

Suddenly suffocated by the crush, Kelda went for a walk. She would be able to leave soon. Tomaso and Daisy weren't going away until tomorrow. She wandered into the drawing-room past several elderly ladies tucking into champagne and talking Italian in staccato bursts of energy. She headed for the conservatory, certain of finding privacy there.

But the conservatory was already very much occupied. Angelo and Fiona were entwined in a passionate embrace beneath the palm trees. Kelda stood on the threshold for several taut, stricken seconds, watching Fiona pushing her fingers through his hair, her lithe body arched into his with the sensual intimacy of lovers who thought they were alone. It was X-certificate stuff and clumsily, slowly, Kelda backed away, her heartbeat pounding unnaturally loudly in her eardrums.

Utterly devastated. That was how she felt. For an insane moment she had wanted to tear their straining bodies apart and impose herself between them. Now wouldn't that have been a novel end to the day? She staggered dizzily into a chair in an alcove off the hall and sat down, hugging herself as though to ward off the intense pain.

Tomaso strode past, paused. 'Have you seen Angelo?'

She jerked a hand wordlessly in the direction of the conservatory, would have liked to say something smart like. 'I think you'll find he's busy,' but could not summon up the poise. She was hurting so much, she didn't think she could bear it without coming apart. She twisted her hands together, battling for control but the pain simply kept on biting at her from new directions.

Inside her head, she saw them together in a far more intimate setting. She squeezed her eyes tight shut in anguish but the image wouldn't leave her alone. She saw them intertwined in passion in tumbled sheets, lying together in the blissful aftermath that once she had known and about there she just wanted to press a button and die.

Someone pulled apart her shaking hands and gripped them tightly in his.

'I'm sorry,' Tomaso said heavily. 'I am very sorry you had to see that.'

The sympathy almost sent her over the edge. She didn't trust herself to speak.

'Kelda...what do you want me to do?'

Her lashes lifted. Her stepfather was hunkered down in front of her, fiercely holding her hands. 'Nothing,' she gasped pleadingly.

'Angelo has the right to know——'

'No, not now!' she forced out painfully. 'I couldn't stand it!'

'You love him.' Tomaso released his breath in a long pent-up hiss, kindly removing his perceptive gaze from her distraught face.

'No...' But even to her own ears it sounded false, empty, a foolish denial of the anguish she was enduring.

Tomaso sighed. 'He would marry you——'

She was appalled by the idea and it showed.

'I would get a car to take you home but you should stay here tonight. I don't like the idea of you being on your own,' her stepfather said quietly.

'I'll be fine.' From somewhere, she got the strength to give him a watery smile. 'I think I need to be on my own.'

Afterwards she couldn't recall a single moment of the drive. She found herself back inside the cottage without quite knowing how she had got there. And then she collapsed, but not into tears. Her eyes burned and ached but not with moisture. She couldn't cry. Tomaso's understanding kindness had almost been her undoing, but now that she was alone all she could do was stare emptily into space.

She *did* love Angelo. Why had she only found that out now, when it was too late to make any difference? But what difference could it ever have made? she asked herself. Six years of bitter misunderstanding lay between her and Angelo, and her own behaviour had only confirmed his opinion of her. Why, oh, why had she set up that scene at her apartment with Russ?

Of course, she hadn't even suspected then that she might be pregnant. But by staging that scene she had finally and most thoroughly confirmed Angelo's low opinion of her morals. There was no way now that she would ever tell Angelo that the baby she carried was his. He despised her but he had found her sexually attractive. That was all it had ever been on his side. Sex. The very last thing on Angelo's mind had been fathering a child.

How could you love and hate someone at the same time? Today she had hated him, but she had loved, wanted and needed him as well with a mindless craving that had shaken her to the very roots of her being.

Jealousy had not touched her until now, but Angelo had plunged her into instant agony. She could not have borne Tomaso's interference in the situation. That, at least, she reminded herself, was no longer likely.

It was after two when she heard a car raking into her driveway. She sat up in bed, listened to the slam of a door, crunching steps on the gravel. The bell went in three sharp, successive bursts.

'Who is it?' she called from the stairs.

'Who the hell do you think?'

Angelo. Weakly she sank down on the second last step. 'Go away!'

'If I have to break in, I'll do it!'

Her breath shortened in her throat. Tying the sash of her robe, she unbolted the door. 'Do you realise what time it is?' she demanded.

'Are you alone?' Angelo sent a slashing glance of suspicion up the stairs.

'What do you want?' Tension held her fast, a nasty flicker of foreboding skimming down her spine. Playing for time to compose herself, she walked into the lounge and switched on a lamp before taking up a stance by the fireplace.

Angelo looked uncharacteristically tousled. His hard jawline was blue-shadowed, his ebony hair ruffled. Although he was still wearing his grey suit, he had discarded his tie and his silk shirt was half unbuttoned. His brilliant dark eyes glittered with a cold menace, accentuated by the rigid tension etched into his striking bonestructure.

'I hear you're pregnant,' he delivered with a soft hiss.

Involuntarily, Kelda recoiled but she made a swift recovery. 'And where did you hear that piece of nonsense?' she managed to toss back boldly.

'Your brother——'

She lost colour. 'T-Tim?'

'He was rather drunk. I gave him a lift back to town,' Angelo divulged with slow, measured emphasis as though he was exercising immense self-control. 'After I'd dropped Fiona off, he began to laugh and crack some rather odd jokes. Your mother asked him to keep an eye on you while she was away and he told me why——'

Not a muscle moved on Kelda's face. 'That doesn't explain what you're doing here at two in the morning——'

'Are you pregnant?' Angelo demanded with ferocious anger.

'I owe you no explanations,' Kelda flung back. 'I don't have to defend myself against Tim's drunken ramblings.'

'In Italy, you said that somehow, some day you would get your own back on me for bringing you there.' The reminder lanced into the smouldering silence. 'If this is it, I'll fight you and I'll break you!' he swore with brutal clarity. 'You've told your mother that you're pregnant. I want to know if you're lying...and if you're not, I want to know now whose child it is!'

Hysteria was fluttering like a wild bird captured in her throat. Her stomach was churning. 'Relax, Angelo...it isn't yours,' she asserted through bloodless lips, holding herself proudly erect only by rigorous discipline.

The silence throbbed. He didn't relax in receipt of her assurance. He went rigid.

'Then why does your brother think it is?' he lashed back at her finally with splintering savagery, every powerful line of his lean body emanating his bitter anger.

'They know about Italy, and before you blame me for that, let me disclaim all responsibility. We were photographed at the airport. Someone sent your father a cutting,' she shared with a tiny tremor in the voice she was fighting to keep level.

Angelo said something raw in Italian and strode over to the window, his back squarely turned to her, scorching tension in the angle of his broad shoulders.

'I assured them that you weren't the culprit,' she muttered tightly, and that at least was true.

'Then who is?'

She made no response. Her wide green eyes were dark with exhaustion and stress.

'Russ Seadon...*si*,' Angelo decided, flicking her a glance of incandescent golden rage and bitterness. 'I did recognise him,' he ground out.

'Good for you,' she mumbled shakily because she didn't have the strength to fight Angelo after the traumas of the past thirty-six hours.

'*Is it his child*?' he demanded, coming back to her in one long, threatening stride. 'I demand to know!'

'You have no right to ask me that,' Kelda snapped, taking a step back from him.

'I want the truth!' Angelo grabbed her wrists with two strong hands and yanked her up against him. 'If it isn't mine, whose is it?'

'Go to hell!' she gasped, struggling to release herself from his fierce grip.

'*Tell me*!' he blazed down at her insistently, his striking bone-structure clenched with dark fury.

From somewhere deep inside her where outrage could pull on final reserves of energy, she found the courage to hurl, 'You see, I didn't pine for you, Angelo! Not for a day or even an hour...'

'You make me understand why men kill.' As Angelo stared down into her flushed and exquisitely delicate face, white hot rage flamed in his piercing gaze. 'I would rather see you buried than swollen with another man's seed,' he admitted through clenched teeth.

Losing every scrap of colour, Kelda momentarily sagged in his fierce grip. She looked at him in horror. 'Are you c-crazy?'

'Obsessed. Does that please you?' Angelo drawled with razor-edged softness. 'I doubt if it does. You want me to stay away, because you're obsessed, too——'

'No!'

'You don't like seeing me with another woman. That hurt,' Angelo savoured with primitive relish. 'You

couldn't hide that from me. Like a knife twisting inside
you. It made you sick. It terrified you——'

Perspiration beaded her brow. 'Don't...I hate you!'

Angelo hauled her even closer, wound a lean hand
possessively into the tangled fall of her hair to hold her
prisoner. 'A couple of centuries ago you'd have been
burnt at the stake for witchcraft, but you can burn in
my bed instead——'

'Let g-go of me!' In disbelief, she could feel her breasts
lifting and swelling in hard collision with his muscular
chest. He brought his other hand down to her hips and
crushed her suggestively into the hard cradle of his
thighs. The thrust of his erection sent excitement
spiralling through her in waves and she squeezed her eyes
tightly shut in wild rejection. 'No...no!'

She would not surrender to that excitement, she told
herself furiously but he lowered his dark head and, instead of the aggressive assault she had expected, he let
his mouth nip teasingly along the fullness of her lower
lip, locking the oxygen in her throat.

'Angelo, please...' Her own voice sounded miles away,
oddly strangled.

'Please what?' He let his tongue delve inch by inch
between her parted lips and the world stood still and her
knees turned to sawdust. Her entire body was pitched
to that single caress.

'Stop,' she moaned.

'But you want this as much as I do.' His tongue flicked
into the sensitive interior of her mouth and she clutched
at him, every muscle jerking tight. He was pushing her
backwards, lifting her off the carpet and then pressing
her back against the wall.

He buried his lips hotly in a hollow of her collarbone
and she trembled violently, her nipples peaking into
painful sensitivity. His hands skimmed down the taut
length of her thighs and she felt him shudder against
her, his heart thundering against her spread fingers, as
madly accelerated as her own.

He cupped the ripe curve of her bottom in his hands and she bit at his shoulder in frustration, what remained of her control evaporating fast.

'Tell me that you're lying,' he urged unsteadily.

'What?' she mumbled, slurring the word, lost in a world of intense sensation that utterly seduced.

'Tell me that you're not pregnant,' Angelo demanded in a roughened, almost pleading undertone.

'But...I am,' she responded on the peak of a sob of unbearable excitement.

'Bitch,' he groaned savagely, and suddenly tore himself back from her.

Kelda opened glazed eyes. Angelo was several feet away, his breathing pattern ruptured and audible. He made no attempt to conceal his blatant physical excitement. He looked back at her while she braced herself with shaking hands against the wall to stay upright. Luminescent gold engulfed her in the implacable force of his will.

'And the baby is not mine...it's definitely not mine?' Angelo persisted roughly, rawly launching the demand at her in raking challenge. 'How can you be so sure it's not?'

In her mind's eye, she saw him with Fiona and the pain and bitterness hit her afresh. To admit the truth would be the ultimate humiliation. 'Definitely not yours,' she spelt out.

He raked something at her in his own language and then spread his hands in a soundless arc of violent anger. 'I am not prepared to live with the reminder that you went to bed with another man after me! If you choose to behave like a whore, *you* take the responsibility for the consequences...I will not! I don't want you with another man's bastard!'

In increasing distress, Kelda put her hands over her ears, lowering her head as a wave of dizziness folded in on her.

Spots swam in front of her eyes. Angelo blurred out of view. She thought she was going to suffocate in the darkness before she passed out and slid down the wall in a faint.

She felt so sick coming to that she was afraid to move a muscle.

'She's coming round,' an unfamiliar voice said witheringly. 'As I said she would. Perhaps if you fed your wife a little more and let her go to bed at a more reasonable hour, she would be somewhat healthier. Pregnant women need extra rest and a sensible diet——'

'Pregnant,' Angelo echoed, not quite steadily, with the same revulsion that might have distinguished a reference to an unmentionable disease.

'If that is your attitude, I can quite see why she's starving herself into a skeleton...what has she had to eat today?'

'The icing off a slice of wedding cake. Nothing else.'

Kelda's eyes opened wide at this instantaneous and correct response. How had Angelo known that? He must have been watching her.

Angelo had called out a doctor. The gentleman in question was balding, beetle-browed and near retirement. He was also treating Angelo to a look of scathing contempt. 'And that didn't bother you?' he demanded.

'I'm fine...sorry you had to be bothered,' Kelda broke in hurriedly and tried to sit up.

The doctor's hand restrained her. 'Stay where you are. I want to see you in my ante-natal clinic Thursday afternoon at two and don't bother bringing your husband. We'll do very well without him.' With that blistering assurance, he took his leave. 'Don't trouble yourself, Mr Rossetti. I can see myself out.'

Long after the cottage door had slammed, the silence stretched. Angelo was poised rigid-backed by the window. He was staring out into the darkness beyond the glass. 'I don't know what I'm doing here,' he admitted with gritted abruptness.

Kelda glanced down at herself and discovered she was attired in one of her mother's frilly cotton nightdresses. Her cheeks flushed. She hadn't been wearing anything under the robe. 'You put this on me——'

'The least of my sins,' Angelo said half under his breath.

'I didn't need a doctor——'

'What was I supposed to do when you collapsed? Step over you and drive off?'

'Yes,' she said sickly, recalling all that had passed before. 'It would have been more in keeping.'

'I was very shocked and confused when I came here tonight. I did not fully consider what I was doing,' Angelo proffered in a murderously controlled tone. 'I should have waited until I had cooled down. Naturally you are pregnant. Why should you lie about such a thing?'

'It doesn't matter.' Kelda was drained, depressed, empty of all reaction.

'What was between us is finished——'

She closed her eyes in sudden pain, registered that she was not after all as empty of emotion as she had imagined. She could not cope with Angelo and she could not cope without him. She didn't know which was worst.

'It *has* to be,' Angelo stressed. 'I could never forget that you went to bed with Seadon after you were with me in Italy——'

Dumbly she shook her head on the pillow.

'I could never accept another man's child in these circumstances. How could you let him touch you after me?' he bit out in sudden slashing challenge.

'I don't want to talk about it.' She turned her head away.

'Are you finally ashamed of yourself when it is too late to make any difference?' he derided half under his breath.

'You could never trust me...all these years, never once have you trusted me or given me the benefit of the doubt,' she condemned helplessly, talking to herself, no longer listening to him. 'I can't handle that, I never could.'

'You won't be expected to handle it from now on.'

'And now for the good news,' she whispered unsteadily.

Dark, dark eyes without a shade of gold rested on her. 'I wanted you so badly, for so long that it was like a sickness in my blood. I was determined to have you at any cost. I thought I could exorcise you with sex but all that achieved was an even greater obsession. I don't like what you do to me,' Angelo confessed, his beautiful mouth thinning into a forbidding line. 'I don't like the way I behave with you. I like to be in control...a hangover from my childhood...I am not in control with you.'

Neither was she, and sometimes, like now, when he was tearing her in two, it was terrifying. She hated him for hurting her, for not loving her, for insulting her, but when it came to the image of him walking out of the door she wanted to trail him back to hurt and insult all over again. The destruction was more bearable than the emptiness.

'Go away!' she suddenly demanded.

Angelo expelled his breath in an audible hiss of rampant frustration. 'You look so fragile and yet you're strong enough to defy me. Even as a child you defied me!'

She had thrust her face into the pillow. 'I needed someone to put their arms round me and make me feel I *belonged*!'

'I couldn't trust myself that close,' Angelo muttered in a stifled tone of self-disgust.

'I wish you'd go.'

'No, you don't...sometimes I know what you feel before you even think it. Who is the father?' he asked again without warning, but this time his wine-dark voice was icily controlled. 'Is it Seadon?'

'Does it matter?'

'I would really prefer not to know for sure,' he admitted harshly.

'Damn you, Angelo!'

'You need to eat something,' he murmured prosaically. 'What do you want?'

'You're insane,' she accused weakly.

'Guilty as hell. You're sick, you're pregnant and your wrists have a full set of my fingerprints on them,' Angelo enumerated curtly. 'How do you expect me to feel?'

He left the room. Shakily, she lifted her wrists into the light and saw the purplish bruising he had inflicted earlier. She hadn't felt any pain at the time. Her fair skin marked easily but feeling a total heel had to be a new sensation for Angelo, and not one that would do him any noticeable harm. He would leave her now and go back to Fiona. Lying had been the right thing to do, she told herself wretchedly. The torturous cycle of destruction inside her would be stopped and she would heal. Angelo would leave her alone.

It took him a long time but eventually he reappeared with a bowl of soup.

They were in a state of temporarily suspended hostilities, she acknowledged. Dawn was breaking outside. She remembered another dawn and her cheeks burned, making her duck her head down and tuck into the soup. The soup was as burnt as her skin. She persevered beneath his taut scrutiny, ridiculously conscious all of a sudden of a desire not to reject even so small an olive branch. In the harsher light, the strain in his darkly handsome visage was pronounced. He looked as savaged as she felt.

The words he had employed came back to haunt her. Sickness... obsession... exorcism. And *sex*. Unhealthy, destructive, debilitating. Not flattering. And what was that hangover from his childhood? He liked to be in control. Scarcely a revelation to anyone in Angelo's radius! Angelo could turn an impromptu picnic into an organised field expedition.

'Why do you have to be in control?'

His eyes veiled. 'I grew up with a woman like you. A free spirit. Any man, any time, any place——'

Like you... She swallowed hard on her angry frustration. 'What woman?'

'My mother. And she wasn't ashamed of it either. My father adored her but he couldn't live with her affairs. That's why he divorced her, but she still got custody of me. I hated the life I had with her. She was suffocatingly possessive and very volatile——'

'So are you.'

Angelo dealt her a chilling half-smile. 'Only with you, and that I can overcome,' he stated with cool conviction. 'I don't want to live on the wild side with any woman. I want a quiet, well-behaved, conservative wife who would die of shock if I made love to her the way I make love to you. At times, she'll bore me... after a few years, I'll be walking out the door and forgetting she exists, and not long after that I will most probably set up a mistress.'

'And I hope like hell your wife throws orgies while you're at the office!' Kelda breathed in a blitz of stormy revulsion and pain.

'You might; she won't. She'll accept the package deal. Many women do. Status, money, children and a husband whose infidelities are discreet.'

'You burnt the soup.' Kelda rolled over, presenting him with her narrow back. Her fingers clawed like talons into the pillow beside her head. She could not deal with such honesty. He was not trying to hurt her. He was telling her what he believed would make him happy...or as happy as he believed he could afford to be and still be one hundred percent in control.

'You should keep that appointment with the doctor. If you need anything——' He hesitated. 'Try not to involve me unless it's an emergency.'

She listened to the car drive off, strained to hear the last distant sounds and then flopped. *He burnt the soup and I ate it.* And she started to laugh like a madwoman until the dragging sobs surfaced and finally she cried, cried for herself alone. Angelo, the Angel of Darkness, who made the City quail, was an emotional coward. A wimp like that wasn't worth her tears, and he wasn't fit to be the father of her child either!

CHAPTER EIGHT

'I've been laughing into my cornflakes every morning this week following Carol Philips' story of life with dear, misunderstood Danny,' Gina said mockingly to the table at large. She looped a straying strand of cornsilk hair from her brow with a beringed hand and giggled. 'He *actually* brought one of his women home to lunch and let her think that his wife was his sister!'

'Carol Philips was a doormat. She got what she asked for,' one of the other women remarked drily. 'I'd have thrown him and his floozy out . . . I wouldn't let any man treat me like that!'

'She had two young children and he kept her very short of money,' Kelda put in quietly. 'She was only eighteen when he married her. She had never had a job. I can understand how trapped she must have felt——'

'Oh, you!' Her friend Gina wrinkled her classic nose. 'How can you feel sorry for Danny's wife after what *he* did to you?'

'I must have hurt her as well,' Kelda pointed out ruefully.

'Even she admitted that you were the only one who dumped him immediately you found out that he was married——'

'And it's cleared your name of all that rubbish that was printed,' Russ commented. 'You came out squeaky clean, compared with all the others the wronged wife chose to name. There's been quite a few red faces on the catwalks this past week!'

Her companions continued to trawl over Carol's revelations, a tabloid exposé which had been running all week and causing more hilarity than anything else. Danny's wife had sold her story because Danny had left her practically destitute when he'd swanned off to New York, taking the children's curvaceous teenage nanny with him.

Kelda pushed back her chair and got up.

'Are you feeling all right?' Gina asked anxiously, searching her pale face.

'I'm off to the cloakroom again... don't draw everybody's attention to it,' Kelda begged with a wry grin.

She was feeling sick, although she was trying to hide the fact. In addition she had a nagging pain in her lower abdomen. It was not the first time that she had experienced such symptoms in recent days. The pain came and went, sometimes only irritating, but on at least one other occasion actually quite painful.

She had meant to make time to go to the doctor but she was quite convinced that she knew what was wrong with her. The thick pregnancy manual she had bought described what was called 'round ligament pain', something to do with the stretching of the ligaments that supported the uterus and nothing to worry about. She would make an appointment at the clinic for the day after tomorrow, she promised herself. Just to be on the safe side.

In the cloakroom she looked at her reflection and made a face. Her cunningly cut, flowing dress concealed the firm swell of her stomach from all but the most intent observers, but she still felt like a beached whale. Seven months pregnant and feeling it, she thought ruefully.

She had kept so busy over the past five months that the time had flown but sometimes, like now, in the middle of a convivial crowd of friends, something that was more than tiredness would swamp her. It was a combination of loneliness, self-pity and emptiness, and she thoroughly despised herself for the weakness. After all, she had been been very lucky and she was not alone, except in the sense that she did not have a supportive male in her life.

Every other day, Tomaso and Daisy were either on the phone or the doorstep, having failed to fulfil Angelo's prophecy that they would spend most of their time abroad. Tim appeared regularly, invariably clutching yet another fluffy toy to add to a steadily growing collection. And, best of all, Russ and Gina had returned to London to set up a modelling agency of their own and tomorrow they were getting married. That was one reason why Kelda had no intention of being a wet blanket.

Her friends had been marvellous. When the first unmistakable signs of her burgeoning stomach had forced her to stop modelling, Russ and Gina had stepped in to offer her a job. Gina was in so much demand as a model that it was impossible for her to devote much time to helping Russ with their agency. Russ, in turn, was either out on a shoot or in the studio. Kelda had been installed to handle the bookings and run the small agency on a day-to-day basis.

She was not rich but she was no longer in debt. She had managed to work long enough to clear all outstanding bills. Then she had cut up her credit cards and returned them, accepting that she had to learn to exist on a much reduced budget until such time as the baby was born. Her hand slid down to her stomach in an unconsciously protective movement. The years ahead would be a struggle and she had faced that reality head-on, but her commitment to her unborn child remained unchanged.

Gina was talking almost fiercely to Russ when Kelda rejoined them. One of those sudden awkward silences fell. 'Do you want me to go away and come back again?' Kelda said only half-jokingly.

'You look tired,' Russ told her abruptly. 'Do you want to go home?'

'Dear Russ...such fabulous tact,' Gina breathed, throwing her fiancé a dirty look. 'Why should Kelda scuttle off home because *he's* here?'

More even-tempered than Gina, Russ sighed. 'I only thought——'

Gina grabbed Kelda's arm. 'Look, there he is over there!'

Kelda didn't want to look. Suddenly she turned cold. Angelo was here. There was only one male capable of rousing Gina to such fury. It had to be Angelo. Sometimes, Kelda wished she hadn't told her friends the truth, but she had known they would be discreet, and a lie which promised to stretch ahead of her year after year had not seemed practical.

'*Lousy, womanising swine*!' Gina hissed in her ear. 'That's Isabel Dunning with him. She's really top-drawer.'

Isabel, Kelda rhymed inwardly, to follow on from Adele, Caroline, Felicity and Fiona. In five months, Angelo had worked through the English upper classes with a fine-tooth comb, but not one of the lovely ladies had lasted. The gossip columnists were agog at such volatile romancing. Then they didn't know what Kelda knew ... Angelo was scouring society for a suitable wife. A conservative wife from a good background with no scandals in her past.

'She'll run to fat in a few years,' Gina said nastily.

Kelda was looking, although she had tried so hard not to. But there was this terrible, wicked craving inside her. She had not seen Angelo in the flesh since that night at the cottage. His partner was slender, blonde, impeccably dressed and distinctly beautiful. And Angelo? The air locked in her throat. A shudder ran through her. Angelo was Angelo. Striking, vital, magnificent. She could not dredge her hungry gaze from him.

'Care to dance?' Russ demanded.

'Yes, go ahead.' Gina gave her a determined push. 'Don't be a wallflower with him around!'

Kelda found herself out on the floor without knowing how she had arrived there. As Russ whirled her around with more enthusiasm than rhythm, she caught flickering glimpses of Angelo. His hard-edged profile...the uncompromising set of his jawline...the sheen of his ebony hair beneath the lights. Had he lost weight or was that only her imagination? Maybe it was the shadows which carved those dark features into leaner, older lines.

Suddenly, she was filled with self-loathing. She was not some lovesick teenager, still longing for some arrogant young male, who had treated her badly! Where was her pride? While she struggled to survive, Angelo had been breaking all known records with a constant stream of other women. And a sixth sense warned her that he might well be announcing his marital plans soon. Angelo, married, introducing her to his wife...she broke out in nervous perspiration.

The imagery summoned up made her feel sick and dizzy. Would Tomaso retain his silence when Angelo brought home a wife-to-be? She was painfully aware that her stepfather was finding that silence harder and harder to maintain. Five months ago he had perhaps hoped that his son and his stepdaughter might reconcile without any interference from him and then all constraint would be at an end within the family circle. But after this length of time Tomaso could no longer sustain such a hope.

'Could we sit down?' she gasped breathlessly.

'Too energetic?' Russ grimaced. 'Sorry, I keep on forgetting...'

I don't, Kelda reflected miserably. Russ curved a supportive arm to her spine and by the worst possible misfortune chose the path back to their table that went closest to Angelo's. They came face to face in the aisle.

'Kelda...' Angelo stilled. Tension thickened the atmosphere but he stared at her with impassive dark eyes, cold as charity. 'What a pleasant surprise,' he drawled. 'Let me introduce you to Isabel...Isabel, this is my stepsister, Kelda——'

'I'm delighted to meet you.' Isabel extended a polite hand.

Stepsister . . . the term, the very word shattered Kelda. Angelo had never used it before. Like a robot, she forced her arm up to meet Isabel's fingers, briefly, loosely connecting and dropping away again.

'And Russ.' Russ's arm tightened round Kelda's rigid back.

'Perhaps Kelda and Russ would like to join us.' As Isabel turned to address Angelo, she rested her left hand on his sleeve and the elegant diamond solitaire on her engagement finger caught the light. 'The more the merrier when one's celebrating, don't you think?' she said with a teasing smile.

'Sorry, we're with a party of our own,' Russ retorted with a distinctly forced smile.

A moment later, Kelda dropped heavily down into her chair, white as a sheet.

'What's wrong?' Gina asked of Russ.

'The bastard just introduced her to his fiancée.'

'Men!' Gina snorted, unlocking the door of her docklands apartment where Kelda was to spend the night. Russ was staying the night with his best man. Gina stalked over to the drinks cabinet. 'You need a brandy. You look like a corpse!'

'No,' Kelda shook her head.

'Not even this once?' Gina wheedled.

'Sorry.'

'Well then, I insist you get straight into bed and I'll bring supper in.'

'Gina, it's only ten——'

'We should have had a hen-night and stayed home,' her friend muttered crossly. 'That club was Russ's idea.'

'I was bound to run into Angelo sooner or later.' With a very real effort, Kelda tilted her chin and managed to smile. 'Don't worry about it.'

'Do you think I came down with the last shower of rain?' Gina enquired very drily. 'You are absolutely devastated!'

Kelda contrived a jerky shrug. 'It was on the cards. So, he's getting married ... so what?'

'You should have told him the truth months ago!'

'Gina!' Kelda was shaken.

Her friend sighed. 'You deliberately drove him away by letting him think that Russ and you were involved——'

'I didn't know I was pregnant——'

'And then you tell him it's not his baby!' Gina recounted.

'Do you really think that he wanted to hear that it was?'

Presented with that angle, Gina winced.

Kelda managed to produce a wry laugh. 'I did the right thing, Gina, and I'm over him. I'm really not martyr material. Plenty more fish in the sea.'

Gina frowned. 'Is that really how you feel?'

'Yes.' Kelda walked into the kitchen. 'Now where is this fancy no-cook supper you promised me, and all the gossip?'

'Have you found out yet who is sending you those luscious hampers every week?'

Kelda smiled. For months she had been receiving luxury hampers of fabulous food from Harrods. 'Tomaso, of course.'

'Your *stepfather*?' Gina exclaimed in comical disappointment. 'I thought you had a secret admirer!'

'Chance would be a fine thing, the shape I'm in.'

'Are you sure it's him?'

'Who else?' Kelda said wryly. 'I taxed him with it and of course he denied it, but he hates being thanked for anything. It has to be him. He was really quite put out with me when I told him I wouldn't accept any financial help from him and Mum.'

Later, as she lay sleepless in Russ and Gina's guest-room, the tears trickled silently down her cheeks into her hair, making her skin burn. As fast as they came, she scrubbed them away. Angelo was getting married.

That was not the end of her world. She could get by without Angelo...hadn't she been doing so for months? Angelo's marriage was merely the last act in a grotesque black comedy.

Why should it upset her? Even if she had told the truth and Angelo had accepted that he was the father of her child...even if he had asked her to marry him, she would have turned him down. She had no doubts about that reality. She might love Angelo in that insane, unreasoning way that women sometimes loved, but she did not *like* Angelo, and literally cringed from the idea of living with him as an unwilling and no doubt unfaithful husband. No, much as it might hurt, Kelda was convinced that her future was far safer solely in her own hands.

The pain in her abdomen came back midway through Russ and Gina's wedding breakfast the following morning. She had to leave the table to be ignominiously sick but she managed to conceal her pallor with judicious use of cosmetics before she returned.

'I think you should go home to bed,' Gina scolded none the less when she was changing out of her unconventional scarlet designer wedding-gown. 'All that standing around for the photos has exhausted you.'

By then, Kelda was feeling pretty awful and just a little scared. The pain was worse. She knew she needed to see a doctor but she was determined not to cloud her friends' wedding-day. Half an hour later, she waved them off and walked back into the hotel, intending to call a cab, but without warning a sliver of absolute agony pierced her. With a stifled cry, she pressed a hand to her stomach. A red mist rose in front of her eyes. She took a staggering step in the direction of a chair but she didn't make it. She collapsed in the foyer.

'If she dies, I'll never forgive you!' Daisy launched across the waiting-room, her pretty face swollen and distraught with tears. 'Have you any idea how dangerous acute appendicitis is at this stage of her pregnancy? They *have* to operate but she might lose the baby! And if she loses that baby, Angelo, I'll never forgive you for that either!'

'Daisy...Daisy,' Tomaso soothed, tugging his almost hysterical wife into his arms. 'Angelo didn't come here for this——'

'Why did he come?' Daisy sobbed into his shoulder. 'What's he doing here *now*?'

'Today Kelda's two closest friends got married,' Angelo informed her tightly. 'That's why I'm here.'

Daisy surveyed him with blank incredulity. 'What has that got to do with anything?'

Kelda came back to consciousness in a strange room. Her throat was unbearably dry and her head ached and she was dully aware that she could feel a different kind of pain now. Thankfully no longer severe, the pain had been reduced to throbbing discomfort instead. There was a nurse bending over her. She focused on her with difficulty. 'Where am I?'

'The recovery-room.'

'Am I recovered?' she mumbled ungrammatically.

'We hope so.'

'My baby?' Kelda whispered shakily, suddenly terrified.

'Hanging in there like a Trojan.' The nurse smiled and blurred again.

The next time Kelda surfaced, she felt a little less removed from the world. Her mother was holding her hand and a nurse was taking her blood-pressure. 'What happened to me?' she whispered.

In a voice thickened by tears, her mother explained. 'Why didn't you go to the doctor?' Daisy scolded finally.

'I meant to.'

'Tomaso wants you to see Angelo,' her mother volunteered reluctantly.

'A-Angelo?' Kelda echoed, attempting to sit up and being firmly pressed back down again by the clucking nurse. 'What's *he* doing here?'

'Do you want to see him?'

Kelda shut her eyes tightly, an expression of weary pain crossing her drawn features. 'No... please, no.'

Kelda turned her face to the wall when she was alone again. Angelo? The very last person she had any desire to see when she was weak and in pain and quite frankly at the end of her tether. What was he doing here? And how dared Tomaso ask her to see him! In the cause of family unity, she supposed and she could see the point of that, even agree with his motivation but *now* was not the time to expect her to rise gracefully above selfish human feelings.

Later, she promised herself, later when she was feeling better and she could congratulate Angelo on his engagement and hopefully *mean* it. Right now, she needed time, time to adjust to that new set of circumstances and detach herself from the milling turmoil of her own confused emotions. And there was no doubt that she was desperately confused. She had honestly believed that she had her emotions under control... she had believed that she had come to terms with the complete impossibility of any relationship with Angelo... she had believed in that acceptance right up until the moment she saw that diamond on Isabel Dunning's hand.

Then her self-deception had been smashed. She had not merely been shocked, she had been agonised by the extent of her own pain and an unexpectedly fierce sense of rejection. And she *had* to learn how to handle those feelings. Her pregnancy had divided the family circle in two. For the past five months Angelo had smoothly avoided her, and their parents had made that relatively easy for them. But that could not go on for much longer without imposing intolerable strain upon Tomaso and Daisy. Somehow, some way, Kelda knew she had to face up to the situation and finally settle it.

In the middle of the night, the staff allowed her to have a cup of tea and a small piece of toast. When the door on her private room widened, she barely glanced up because the nurses had been in and out constantly throughout the night, checking up on her. She focused on a pair of male trousered legs and slowly angled her head back against the pillow. Her heart jumped into her mouth.

'I persuaded them to let me in,' Angelo revealed in a taut, uncharacteristic rush as though he was determined to get in first vocally. 'I've been here all day.'

He was poised just inside the door and, if she stared, it was because she didn't know Angelo like this. Badly in need of a shave, crumpled, tousled and very pale. Harsh lines of strain were grooved between his nose and mouth. His lustrous dark eyes were curiously unguarded as they rested on her. He released his breath in an audible hiss and his dark gaze wandered slowly and almost carefully over her.

'I don't want you here,' she whispered, and closed her eyes, shutting him out.

'I needed to see you...' The admission was rough-edged.

'Why?' she sighed.

'How can you ask me that?' he demanded in an incredulous undertone, abruptly sounding more like himself. 'The child you carry is *mine*——'

Kelda's lashes lifted. She studied him in sudden sharp distress, her every muscle tensing as though she was under attack. 'Where did you get that idea?'

'Well, certainly not from you,' Angelo responded with fierce emphasis.

'I don't know what you're talking about,' she said weakly, playing for time, wondering in despair if in the heat of her collapse Tomaso and Daisy had betrayed their knowledge.

'How could you think you could get away with a lie like that?' Angelo demanded in a low-pitched growl.

'Sooner or later, I would have found out. Russ Seadon and Gina Delfont are your two closest friends. You have never been involved with Seadon. Your name has never been linked with his and yesterday you played a starring role in their wedding.'

'And where did you get all this information?' she prompted unsteadily.

'Her bloody dress featured on the lunchtime news!' Angelo launched at her with sardonic bite. 'I was already trying to get hold of you yesterday when my father called me to tell me that you were in hospital. Don't try to tell me that you were sleeping with Seadon five months ago behind your best friend's back...I wouldn't believe you!'

'I never said that Russ was the father of my child,' Kelda muttered shakily.

'But you repeatedly denied that *I* was,' he reminded her doggedly. 'And that night at your apartment when he came out of the bedroom, you made no attempt to explain the situation——'

Kelda turned her face to the wall, filled by sudden expected guilt for the scene she had sprung on him. Apparently he had as yet no suspicion that she had deliberately manufactured that scene. That knowledge would have told him just how vulnerable she had felt herself to be all those months ago. But how long would it take for him to recall Russ's exact behaviour that night? Russ had not acted like a platonic friend.

'Why *should* I have tried to explain the situation?' she enquired, still unable to meet his eyes.

'If you cannot answer that, I refuse to answer it for you,' Angelo responded with a dark, driven bitterness that burned. 'The night I came to the cottage——'

'You came through the door in a rage!' Kelda condemned with equal bitterness. 'And you wanted me to deny that I was pregnant——'

'I did not behave rationally that night,' Angelo breathed tautly.

'Actually I think you were very rational,' Kelda muttered flatly, unable to look at him although she could feel his enervating presence with every fibre of her body. 'The very idea of my being pregnant with your child was your worst nightmare come true. You accused me of deliberately trying to set you up——'

'In the heat of temper,' Angelo inserted with raw emphasis. 'Try to put yourself in my position!'

'No, thank you. I'm more concerned with my own,' she said honestly. 'It would have saved everyone a lot of trouble if I'd been able to stick to the stranger-at-a-party fiction. I'm afraid I just wasn't prepared to be faced with the fact that your father knew we had been in Italy together.'

'The idea of your being pregnant with my child would not have been my worst nightmare come true . . .' Angelo stated flatly, unemotionally, as if he had all his feelings under strict lock and key.

The silence stretched. Kelda made no comment. She didn't believe him. Now that he knew the truth, he felt that he had to defend himself from such a charge.

'I find it very hard to accept that all these months everyone *but* me has known the truth,' Angelo continued grimly. 'How did you prevail upon my own father to keep quiet?'

'He saw you in the conservatory with Fiona and, being slightly more sensitive than you are capable of being, understood why I had no wish for you to know.' As she spoke, she rolled her head on the pillow, fixing huge shadowed green eyes on him with unhidden scorn.

Dark colour had sprung up in a line over his striking cheekbones. He had the rail at the foot of the bed between his lean hands and so fierce was the grip that she could see the whiteness of his knuckles shining through his brown skin. 'How could I have known you were pregnant?' It was a rare plea for understanding.

'You didn't much care either way,' Kelda retorted, fighting against the tremendous tiredness sweeping over her.

'That isn't true,' he argued rawly.

'It really doesn't matter now.' Her weary voice slurred the syllables, her eyelids lowering without her volition. 'All water under the bridge, not worth tussling about——'

'Not *worth*——?' Angelo bit off whatever he had intended to say with visible difficulty. 'How can you say that? If you had been alone at the cottage today, you would have died and my child with you!' he said with restrained ferocity, incandescent golden eyes flaming over her pale but now intent face. 'It was the merest good fortune that you collapsed in a public place. So don't tell me that what I feel now doesn't matter!'

He had shaken her, but still her long feathery lashes drifted down. She shifted uncomfortably on the pillows, her hair trapped below her shoulders. Somebody gently slid a hand beneath her spine and tugged the recalcitrant strands of red-gold across her slight shoulders. 'Thanks,' she mumbled, and slept.

After breakfast the next morning, the flowers were delivered. Great drifts of headily scented blooms that filled half a dozen vases and brightened her smart but serviceable surroundings. Her first visitor was her mother.

Daisy was wreathed with smiles. 'I see Angelo's flowers have arrived.'

'Angelo? I assumed you——'

'Well, I was going to, but when I overheard Angelo ordering them on the phone I decided to leave it to another day.'

Kelda, propped up against her banked pillows, was rigid. 'Why would Angelo send me flowers?'

Daisy opened her eyes very wide. 'Can you think of anyone else with more reason?'

'Reason? What reason?' Kelda demanded shakily.

Her mother sat down. 'When Tomaso called Angelo yesterday and told him that you were having emergency surgery, I was angry. When Angelo arrived, I was very upset...well, I said some pretty unforgivable things,' Daisy confided. 'All these months, you've been alone and he's been running round like Casanova——'

Kelda bit the soft underside of her lower lip and tasted blood.

'But here in this hospital yesterday, Angelo was distraught,' Daisy asserted quietly. 'Really, genuinely frantic with worry about you and the baby. I've never seen Angelo like that before. I never realised how emotional Angelo really is underneath the cool front. Tomaso always said he was but I have to admit that I thought that was the fond father talking. Well, as you can imagine, while we were waiting to hear how your surgery had gone, it was a very tense time——'

'Yes?' As her mother's delivery slowed up, Kelda prodded her on, prickles of foreboding tightening her muscles.

'We didn't interfere.' Daisy had stood up again, clearly becoming uncomfortable under the onslaught of her daughter's strained gaze. 'But when it emerged that you had actually told Angelo that your baby *wasn't* his, well, naturally Tomaso and I were very shocked——'

'Naturally,' Kelda repeated in a flattened whisper.

'How could you lie to him like that?' Her mother asked without comprehension. 'We tried to accept that you were both adults and that you knew what you were doing but of course we assumed that, when your pregnancy started to show, Angelo would hear about it and go to see you and things would be sorted out. Thank goodness, Angelo had enough intelligence to realise that you had been lying——'

'Clever Angelo,' Kelda muttered tightly, thinking that she would be hearing about Saint Angelo next. She was now the baddie in this scenario. Angelo now stood absolved of all insensitivity towards her plight in recent times. Then their parents were so innocent. They did not have a clue that Angelo's sole ambition seven months ago had been to buy her into bed and establish her as his mistress.

'I want what's best for you and the baby,' Daisy emphasised.

'I already have what's best,' Kelda said woodenly.

'Angelo had breakfast with us and then he went to bed for a couple of hours. He'll be in later. He says that you're getting married——'

'Does he indeed?' Kelda's pale complexion was consumed by hot colour. Angelo says... her mother had reeled that off with the same naïve faith as she so frequently resorted to 'Tomaso says...' When the males in Daisy's life spoke, she endowed them with oracle-like brilliance.

'I can't tell you how happy we are——'

'He hasn't asked me yet.' Kelda pushed out the admission through clenched teeth.

Her mother's gentle eyes rested rather unfortunately on the swell of Kelda's stomach and then flicked up to her daughter's burning face. 'You're hardly going to say no, are you?' she said, not with satire but with gentle conviction that no woman in Kelda's position could possibly say no to a respectable proposal.

'Mother, Angelo has just got engaged to Isabel Dunning——'

'Don't be silly. Isabel is engaged to his personal assistant, Roger Bamford,' Daisy contradicted with amusement. 'Actually Roger isn't his PA now. Angelo promoted him and now the Dunnings are a bit happier about accepting Roger into the family.'

Wide green eyes blinked at her bewilderment. 'But——'

'All's well that ends well,' Daisy murmured cheerfully, determined to ignore her daughter's response to the good news.

Kelda gritted her teeth and said nothing. It didn't matter whether Angelo was engaged or not. It made no difference. She was outraged that Angelo could calmly inform their parents that they were getting married without even mentioning the idea to her first. It was a subtle form of blackmail and not one which would profit him. She had not the smallest intention of being married off for the sake of appearances.

It was late afternoon when Angelo strolled in. Superbly turned out in a navy suit complete with fitted waistcoat and chain, he looked dressed to kill. He also looked so gorgeous that the nurse, engaged in taking Kelda's blood-pressure, kept on pumping and nearly cut off the blood supply to her patient's arm. Frozen with frank admiration, she stared.

'How are you?' Angelo asked in his rich, slightly accented drawl.

Something wild quivered momentarily deep down inside Kelda as she collided with his clear golden eyes. Resolutely she suppressed it as the nurse took her reluctant leave. 'Fine.'

'We'll get married as soon as you are out of here,' Angelo imparted with studied casualness.

Silence . . . cue for applause, she wondered or was he expecting her to leap from her hospital bed and embrace his knees with gratitude.

Like someone engaged in a high-rolling poker game, Angelo's keen gaze probed her exquisite face. 'We'll stick it out for about six months after the baby's born,' he murmured silkily. 'Then we'll have one or two loud disagreements. You could possibly contrive to run home to Mummy once or twice. We separate . . . we divorce but on a civilised basis, pleading mutual incompatibility. The family will be disappointed but two priorities will have been met. The baby will have my name and everyone will be happy. What do you think?'

CHAPTER NINE

KELDA, trapped humiliatingly between rage and disbelief, had found herself hanging helplessly on his every word. Sizzling emerald eyes rested on his starkly handsome dark features. 'Do you really want to know what I think?'

'I do appreciate that this has come as something of a surprise,' Angelo fielded with teeth-clenching arrogance and the most extraordinary smile playing about his sensual mouth. 'So, I'll leave you to mull it over, shall I?'

With a blind, shaking hand, Kelda swiped the vase of flowers off the bedside cabinet and threw it at him with a strength born of uncontrollable rage. That he neatly sidestepped the deluge did nothing to calm her down. 'You take your flowers, your bloody priorities and your proposal and get out!' she shrieked at the top of her voice. 'I didn't want to be your mistress but I want to be your wife even less and that's saying something! If you got down on your knees and begged for the next twenty years, I wouldn't say yes... so go and ask Adele or Caroline or Felicity... and don't forget Fiona! She does for conservatories what Jayne Mansfield did for sweaters!'

'I'll come back this evening,' Angelo drawled, astonishingly unconcerned by the reception he had received.

'Get out of here,' Kelda raged at him, 'and don't you dare come back!'

Sobbing with a wild mixture of emotions, Kelda was crawling awkwardly about the floor, picking up flowers, when the nurse came in. It hurt, and that only made her angrier.

'Miss Wyatt!' the nurse gasped. 'What are you doing out of bed?'

'Don't let that man in here again!' Kelda hissed, letting herself be assisted back into bed. 'I can't stand him!'

'Was it something he said?'

'Yes...no...oh, I don't know!' Kelda subsided in a damp heap, exhausted by her own loss of control.

'He couldn't have meant it,' the little nurse said shyly. 'My friend told me that he spent half of last night in the chapel. He must have been praying for you.'

Angelo, praying? Kelda could not imagine Angelo praying. She sniffed, had a tissue thrust helpfully into her hand. She had been propositioned with a divorce and even though she would not have agreed to marrying him in any circumstances that had been particularly hurtful.

What did it matter if the baby had his name? Why should she have to consider other people's happiness when she was so wretchedly unhappy herself? And to suggest that putting their parents through the distress of watching their fake marriage disintegrate within months was kinder than never marrying at all was ridiculous! She wanted to be open and honest. No more deception. How dared he expect her to agree to such a proposal...how dared he?

Angelo strolled in after tea as though nothing had happened. Kelda couldn't believe her eyes. He had shed his formal suit. In an oatmeal sweater that highlighted his darkness and close-fitting black jeans that hugged his lean muscular thighs, he looked soul-destroyingly spectacular.

Excitement burned through her nerve-endings, speeding up her heartbeat and sending her pulse-rate racing. She drew in a sharp, deep breath, battling in alarm against the surging tide of dangerous physical awareness.

'This morning I believed that I was suggesting the only kind of marriage that you would even consider,' Angelo imparted with unalloyed cool. 'I know how you feel about me.'

Kelda pushed unsteady hands in a raking motion through her torrent of curls. 'Do you?'

'Why didn't you tell me that Russ Seadon was getting married to your best friend?' he asked without warning.

She tilted her chin. 'Would you have believed me?'

'I don't think that's why you didn't choose to enlighten me,' Angelo fielded. 'I think you felt cornered and he was a good excuse to employ when I jumped to the wrong conclusion.'

'I didn't need an excuse. It wasn't important enough for me to feel I should explain myself,' Kelda told him carelessly.

A muscle jerked beside his unsmiling mouth. 'You didn't care what I thought?'

'It wasn't anything different from what you've thought so often before.'

'But these days you don't mind actually encouraging me to misjudge you...in fact, you get something of a high out of it!'

The condemnation roused colour in her cheeks.

Angelo scrutinised her with impassive eyes. 'And when he strolled out on to centre stage in that towel it was just too convenient for words...'

Every muscle in her body tensed. Striving to look blank, she stared back at him.

'You asked him to play ham, didn't you? It was pre-arranged,' Angelo essayed

Kelda decided defiance was the better part of valour. 'So what if I did? I wanted you out of my life again!'

He was pale beneath his bronzed skin, his dark eyes hooded. 'Game-playing is dangerous in relationships, *cara*.'

'I wouldn't dignify what we shared with the label of "relationship",' Kelda responded tightly. 'Men like you don't have relationships with their mistresses.'

'*Dio*...I've never had a mistress!' Angelo slashed back at her with sudden frustration. 'Do you remember cutting me dead that first night? Do you remember challenging me later in your apartment? Do you remember letting me believe that you would continue to come between our parents? Or was all that my imagination?'

Kelda had stiffened under attack. 'No but——'

'You drove me over the edge that night and you meant to do it,' he condemned.

'I certainly didn't ask to be lured out to Italy——'

'Where you had a hell of a good time in spite of all your complaints——'

'I did not enjoy being arrested and locked up!'

'But you had no complaints about what followed,' Angelo murmured softly.

That was unarguable. He had hit her on her weakest flank. Involuntarily she reddened, her undisciplined mind suddenly awash with erotic recollections. She bent her head. 'I have no desire to talk about that——'

'*That* is unfortunate, considering that your present—condition,' he selected smoothly, 'relates to mutual passion and an outstanding lack of common sense.'

'Is the lack of common sense laid at my door or yours?' she sniped hotly.

'I should think entirely at mine,' Angelo sighed, languorous dark eyes uncomfortably intent on her. 'Considering that I was the idiot who grossly over-estimated the extent of your sexual experience——'

Kelda very nearly dropped the glass of water in her hand. Her head shot up, fiery hair springing back from her disconcerted face.

Angelo dealt her a searching glance and then strolled gracefully over to the window. 'In Italy, I was still hung up on six years of bitterness. Your near-death experience yesterday may not have done much for you but, believe me, it focused my intelligence as never before on all the inconsistencies between rumour and reality. And the reality is that you have not had that many lovers...'

Kelda was appalled by what he was saying. Her brittle front of sophistication and bitchiness was her sole defence against Angelo. And he was coolly ripping it to shreds. Yet her pride depended on that front. She could not bear the idea that Angelo should even come close to suspecting that she was less experienced with men than he had assumed.

'And even now, when we have so many more *important* matters to deal with,' Angelo essayed drily, 'you're wondering how to overturn my assumptions because I have come painfully close to blowing your mystique right out of the water! In my opinion, you hadn't had a recent lover and I assume that you were not taking any contraception either——'

'Contraception fails sometimes,' Kelda responded with rich sarcasm.

Angelo shot her a glittering glance of naked perception. 'You may be the most passionate woman I have ever shared a bed with, but a woman who slept around with the generosity you suggest would have demonstrated practised skills that you did not——'

Her humiliation plumbed new depths. Her eyes blazing, her generous mouth flattened into a strained line, she snapped, 'Shut up!'

Angelo ignored the invitation. 'And because I rejoice in being equally obstinate, I persisted in holding on to my original opinion of your character even in the face of overwhelming evidence to the contrary.'

'Have you finished?'

Angelo took a deep breath and then swore. 'I am trying to say sorry, but you don't make that easy.'

Sorry was even less welcome than the most base of insults from his corner. Kelda ground her teeth together. 'Sorry for what?'

'For all this.' Angelo spread lean brown hands wide with in-bred elegance of movement. 'It's all my fault. I started it——'

'Finished it——' Kelda heard herself remind him.

'It didn't finish for me,' Angelo surveyed her with unreadable hooded eyes, his attention sliding almost compulsively to the visible swell of her abdomen beneath the bedclothes. 'And it isn't finished for you either.'

Kelda dealt him an outraged stare. 'Stop looking at me like that!'

'I like looking at you now...now that I know the baby is mine,' Angelo proffered without a shade of embarrassment. 'Five months ago that baby seemed like an unbridgeable barrier between us. But now it is a link that nothing can break. I wish you could have told me the truth then. If you had, I would have been with you. I never thought of having a child before but, since yesterday, I haven't been able to think of anything else.'

The truth of that confession was blatant. Kelda, hectically flushed, raised her knees slightly and rearranged the bedding to conceal the evidence of her fertility as best she could. A link that nothing could break, he said. She had refused to appreciate that fact before.

'Don't you think that for the sake of the baby we could live together?' Angelo demanded with sudden unconcealed impatience.

'Certainly not. I couldn't stand it!' she slung back at him, hot moisture scalding her eyelids.

'I offered the divorce as what you might term a sweetener to the deal,' Angelo admitted.

'Some sweetener!' Kelda muttered, pleating the sheet with restive fingers.

'You wouldn't need to feel trapped. I would give you a divorce at any time if you asked for one——'

'Angelo, when I want a discreetly unfaithful rich husband in place of my peaceful independence and freedom, I'll advertise! The idea of marrying you,' Kelda framed, fighting the tremor in her thickened voice, 'well, it appeals to me about as much as twenty years of hard labour in a swamp with no time off for good behaviour.'

Angelo had moved forward. The atmosphere vibrated with tension. Refusing to be inhibited by his proximity, Kelda surveyed him with a provocatively curled lip.

'With you in my bed, I would not be unfaithful.'

Kelda sent him a winging glance of forced amusement although her spinal cord had tightened up another notch. 'But I'm not going to be in your bed ever again, Angelo.'

'You want to lay a bet on that?' Angelo sank down on the edge of her bed, shimmering golden eyes ruthlessly pinned her. 'I look at you and you burn. I touch you and you go up in flames. You carry my child inside you. If I branded you with my name, you couldn't be more mine!'

'You arrogant sw——' Kelda began to spit.

Angelo reached for her in one powerful movement. Deftly angling his body to one side so that he would not hurt her, he took her mouth in a devouring kiss that she felt right down to her toes and back up again. She reacted like a woman possessed. With one hand she hit out at him in blind rage, but the other hand inexplicably dived into the springy depths of his hair, holding him to her.

He kissed her breathless. Great rolling waves of excitement overwhelmed her. The hand that had balled into a fist uncurled and slid under his sweater instead and exulted in the satin-smooth skin of his back before sliding across his taut flat stomach to rake into the furrow of silky hair that disappeared beneath his belt.

Angelo jerked violently against her and grabbed her hand, pushing her fingers in an unrestrained expression of need down to the thrust of his hard thighs. He groaned, swore against her mouth, momentarily stiffened as though he was striving to will himself into a withdrawal, and then gathered her fully into his arms with a stifled sound of all male satisfaction.

A loud knock sounded on the door. Angelo sprang off the bed, drove an unsteady hand through his wildly tousled black hair and shot Kelda a glittering glance of mingled frustration and grudging amusement.

Kelda was stricken when Daisy and Tomaso strolled in.

Her stepfather dealt both of them a satiric smile. 'I assume that congratulations are in order.'

'I should think so too,' Daisy teased.

Kelda could feel a painful flush engulfing her skin. Evidently the knock that had been heard had not been the first interruption. She remembered her stepfather saying that he wouldn't trust either of them in the same room for an hour. She remembered the last time they had been surprised on a bed. She burned hotter than ever.

'Congratulations would be premature,' Angelo delivered lazily.

'Kelda!' Her mother exclaimed reproachfully.

'It's my decision.' Embarrassed as she was, Kelda was still strong enough not to be browbeaten by opinion into a corner.

'I want to talk to Kelda alone,' Daisy asserted sharply.

'I don't think that would be a good idea,' Angelo intervened on her behalf, startling her.

The visit was short and sweet. Daisy, whose quiet temperament was only rarely stirred to anger, waited until Angelo had walked out of the door with his father before darting back and positively hissing, 'In my day, you married a man you couldn't keep your hands off... at least if you were lucky enough to be free! You're cutting off your nose to spite your face. I'm sorry but I have to say it. If I don't, who else will?'

'Me?'

Kelda jerked and her mother spun in dismay. Angelo cast them both a slow, splintering smile that did something utterly unforgivable to Kelda's already shaken composure. Daisy reddened and went into retreat.

Angelo studied Kelda from the foot of the bed. 'I'll see you tomorrow.'

'There's no point. I don't want you visiting me.'

When the door closed behind him, she felt incredibly, childishly lonely. She lay back and the baby chose that moment to kick and squirm. She smoothed a possessive and tender hand over her stomach. It was so stupid to love Angelo! If it had been within her power, she would have torn that love out brutally by the roots. She had tried to do that in recent months, had thought she was on the road to recovery...had learnt her mistake all over again.

Angelo was ruthlessly set on building bridges to pave the bridal path, but she couldn't marry him. He didn't seem to realise that no woman with any pride wanted to be married *solely* because an unplanned baby was on the way. Times had changed since her mother's day. Women didn't have to be forced into marriage to save their reputations any more.

Tomaso had undoubtedly made Angelo feel that he *had* to marry her. That was so degrading. She didn't need that pressure. She resented Angelo for giving way to such old-fashioned attitudes but, dismayingly, she suddenly realised that she would resent him even more if he ever chose to marry anyone else. And that was far from a logical attitude considering that she was not prepared to marry him herself.

She found her thoughts returning several times over to something that her mother had said. One of those careless statements which people made in temper without realising how much they were revealing. Daisy had said that in her day you married a man you couldn't keep your hands off...at least if you were lucky enough to be free!

There had been a bitter edge to that assurance. Kelda was shaken when she realised what she had found so disturbing about those words. They were her mother's acknowledgement that once she had been attracted to someone while she was married. Or had they been an acknowledgement of something more than mere attraction? Kelda frowned, angry with herself for thinking in such a way of her own mother. Her mother had adored her father, absolutely adored him, she reminded herself.

Angelo arrived the next day with magazines, books and two boxed sets of nightwear. 'You have no right to buy me that sort of stuff,' she objected.

'Relax ... Harrods maternity department inspired me with no improper thoughts.'

'Maternity department?'

'I hate to tell you this, but you wouldn't make it into anything that didn't come from that department.'

She saw the size on the uppermost box and almost choked on her chagrin. It would have fitted an elephant, never mind a pregnant size eight. Her bottom lip wobbled. Her throat tightened. She studied her stomach with loathing and burst into floods of tears. 'Go away and leave me alone!' she sobbed.

'What did I say?' Angelo endeavoured to put his arms round her but she pulled away.

'Nothing!'

He got a nurse. The nurse came in to soothe, couldn't resist trying to interest her in the contents of the boxes and lifted out the enormous négligé set. 'Is this for you?' she demanded in a choked voice and went off into gales of laughter. 'Didn't anyone tell him that you buy the same size in maternity wear as you wore before you expanded?'

Kelda sat up and blew her nose. 'It would fit an elephant.'

'It would fit two elephants!' She called in two of the other nurses. Kelda's bed was swiftly surrounded by giggling women, bonded by the joy of sheer male ignorance. Kelda began laughing so hard it hurt. She was picturing Angelo in the maternity department, Angelo, who was quite incapable of acknowledging ignorance in any form.

Daisy offered to change them that afternoon. Kelda thought Angelo might visit her again in the evening. He didn't. She thought he might phone. He didn't. Since she had taken the trouble to put on one of the night-dresses, a now correctly sized version courtesy of her mother, she was irritated. She had wanted to share the joke with him. That was all, she told herself, watching the television with flat, disappointed eyes.

She waited for him in the morning. He didn't show. When Tomaso and Daisy rolled up, she was tempted to ask where he was but she fought the temptation. She didn't want to risk rousing the suspicion that she cared whether he came to visit or not. She didn't care. It was just that lying flat on her back with very little exercise was boring and, whatever other faults Angelo had, being boring was not one of them.

She drifted off into a doze at about ten and then a slight sound awakened her. Angelo was poised at the foot of the bed in a dinner jacket and bow-tie. Oddly enough, the sight was like a red rag to a bull. Kelda sat up. 'Where the hell have you been?' she demanded fiercely.

'You missed me...you noticed I wasn't there?' Angelo launched a sizzlingly provocative smile at her, dark eyes glinting like polished jet over her angry face.

'I did not miss you!'

'Obviously you did.'

'I'm stuck in here while you're out there enjoying yourself,' Kelda slung mutinously. 'That makes me sick!'

'My visit upset you so much yesterday, I decided to give you some space,' Angelo revealed flatly.

'Where were you tonight?' She *had* to know. She couldn't get past that raging need to know where he had been and who he had been with.

'At a charity dinner, full of long overblown speeches and pompous old windbags.'

Unexpectedly, she laughed. She told him about the mistake he had made with the lingerie. It was almost the first time she had ever seen Angelo look embarrassed. Suddenly uneasy with the sense of intimacy she was experiencing, she fell silent.

'You're doing it again...shutting me out,' he breathed with a raw edge to his voice. 'I hate it when you do that.'

'I keep on waiting for you to turn on me again.' She had not meant to be that honest but somehow the admission slid out.

He tensed, paled, dark eyes veiling as he paced restively across the room. 'It's taken me a long time but believe me...I've changed. Unfortunately for you, my misconceptions about your temperament were set in concrete that night six years ago——'

Kelda froze in dismay. 'I don't want to talk about that.'

'You had to almost die before I could be forced into facing the truth,' Angelo vented harshly. 'I was afraid of finding myself in a relationship which I couldn't control. I know what that did to my father. I was determined that no woman would do to me what my mother did to him. It was easier to walk away from you than stay...'

Kelda tore her eyes from his clenched profile, knowing what that confession of vulnerability must have cost him.

'Six years ago, I lost control,' he admitted fiercely. 'I overreacted that night. I was hardly an unprejudiced bystander. Even had you been making love with that boy, you would only have been doing what teenagers do, given the opportunity. No, I was brutal with you because I wanted you for myself and the sight of you with that boy drove me crazy——'

'Angelo——'

He cut in on her. 'I was almost twenty-six and you were eighteen. It was almost a year since I had seen you. I had deliberately stayed away. And I came home with such high hopes——'

'What kind of hopes?' She was remembering the way he had looked at her before that ghastly party, his unfamiliar warmth...the compliment.

'I thought that finally I might have a chance with you. Until then, I had had to repress everything I felt around you. Telling myself that I would marry you didn't make me any less ashamed of feeling like that. If you hadn't been so naïve, you would have guessed why I never, ever touched you in any way. You would have questioned the extent of my interest in your education and the amount of freedom you were allowed.'

'I didn't,' she whispered dazedly.

'I have a jealous, possessive streak a mile wide,' Angelo admitted grimly. 'Every time you went out of the door, I went through hell. I knew you ought to have all the normal adolescent experiences but I didn't want you to have them. That's why I had to leave for that year but that night, seeing you with that boy...I went off at the deep end. And now I have to live with the knowledge that you were almost raped. I not only added to your distress by my accusations but also gave way to my own animal instincts in a way which I deeply regret.'

Jealousy had been the source of his incomprehension that night. She saw that now so clearly. Almost immediately her memories of those fevered minutes in his arms were curiously cleansed of all humiliation and embarrassment. If she had been out of control, Angelo had been as well.

'I went to your room to make you listen to the truth, but somehow...' Kelda hesitated awkwardly.

'I opened my eyes and you were there. I thought you had come to me. I didn't remember what had happened earlier until afterwards...and then I believed that you had guessed how I felt and were taunting me,' he breathed savagely. 'But I should never have touched you. I had no excuse.'

Kelda plucked at the sheet. 'I enjoyed it. That devastated me.'

'Do you still feel that I'm about to turn on you?'

She didn't. But she didn't say so. Angelo had changed and she could not understand or even quite accept that Angelo could so suddenly revise his opinion of her. He had given her a completely clean sheet. A mean, jealous streak a mile wide, yes, well, she pondered helplessly, he hadn't been exaggerating on that count. She discovered that she had forgiven him for that night six years ago and that shook her.

But there was something so incredibly appealing about his acknowledgement about how he had felt about her then. True, it had only been rampant sexual desire but he had not intended to take advantage of her innocence. And the more he reminded her of that physical obsession, the more secretively secure she felt. In one sense, Angelo belonged to her. For more than six years, Angelo had continued to desire her. And for more than six years, Angelo, being Angelo, must have fought that hunger to the last ditch... yet still it persisted.

'I won't misjudge you again. I can safely promise you that.' Strong resolve hardened his dark features. 'You say you won't marry me. But have you thought about the future? Whether you like it or not, we'll have a child we have to share within a few weeks...'

Kelda swallowed with difficulty. 'Share?'

'Naturally I will expect to spend time with our child. Even the law would grant me visitation rights, but I doubt if either one of us wants or sees the need for legal intervention,' Angelo stated softly. 'The very existence of that child means that I will be a part of your life for years to come.'

Kelda studied her tightly linked hands. That aspect of the future hadn't occurred to her. Angelo was not disclaiming responsibility. Angelo was telling her up-front that he intended to be there in their lives. Shakenly, she attempted to envisage a purely platonic and civilised relationship with Angelo, the eventual introduction of his lovers into their child's life. Thousands of women had to endure similar situations for the sake of their children's security. But she *loved* Angelo. And Angelo had given her a choice. He had asked her to marry him.

'Couldn't you try being married to me?' Angelo proffered smoothly. 'Couldn't we at least give marriage a chance?'

'I don't want to get married because our parents think we should!' Kelda said.

Incredulity blazed in his eyes. 'What the hell do they have to do with it?' he demanded.

Kelda flinched. 'They want——'

'I'm talking about what I want,' Angelo emphasised drily. 'And I am long past the age of being influenced by what my father wants. Six years ago, he wanted me to marry you and I refused——'

'That night...' she registered with sudden understanding.

'Yes. All would have been instantly forgiven had I been willing to do what he saw as the "decent thing",' Angelo told her. 'But nobody makes me do anything I don't want to do.'

The assurance hung there in the throbbing silence.

'It wouldn't work,' she said tautly.

'How can you say that without giving it a chance?'

'Well, I can't, but how could it?'

'That doesn't mean we can't try. What does trying cost you?'

More pain, more hurt, but would it be any worse than watching him with other women, being forced to share her child with him whenever he made that demand? Wasn't she simply running scared? Riven with raw tension and uncertainty, she cast him an involuntary glance and surprised the same tension in him. He wanted her *and* he wanted the baby. Marriages had survived on considerably less.

'I am not going to beg,' Angelo slung at her.

'I'll marry you.' The instant she surrendered, doubts rushed in and her brow furrowed with anxious lines. 'After the baby's born——'

Angelo threw her a scorching look of anger. 'No!'

'Why not?'

'I'm not prepared to wait. You might change your mind.'

Her teeth ground together but she was very tired. Angelo, she registered, had a lot in common with water dripping on stone. He was incredibly persistent. She rested her head back. 'OK,' she muttered finally.

It was three weeks before Kelda was discharged from hospital. Her blood-pressure had for a time given cause for concern. Forty-eight hours after Tomaso and Daisy took her home with them, Angelo and Kelda were married in the small local church with only family present.

She found the ceremony curiously unreal. Once she had agreed to marry him, Angelo had visited her every day. He had done all the things expected of him. He had brought her gifts, filled her room with flowers and entertained her when her spirits were low. But in spite of that she felt as though he had distanced himself from her. There were no intimacies, no kisses, no hot looks. Angelo held himself aloof and Kelda, ever sensitive to the threat of rejection, was incapable of attempting to bridge the gulf opening up between them.

On their wedding day, she realised that she couldn't see her feet any more, but she told herself bracingly that that scarcely mattered. Angelo was clearly not attracted to very pregnant women. She could accept that, she could live with that, she assured herself. But the awareness that her sole attraction for Angelo was physical and that that sole attraction had vanished along with her feet and her once tiny waist made her feel more insecure than ever.

She wanted to shrink behind Angelo when they emerged from the church and discovered a barrage of cameras awaiting them. The media had finally found out about them and there was no greater joy for a tabloid than to publish pictures of a groom with an eight-month-pregnant bride, especially when the groom had been very publically romancing other women for most of that same pregnancy.

Kelda was trembling when they drove off in a chauffeur-driven limo. For the first time in her life she had felt threatened by a camera lens. Angelo covered her tightly gripped hands soothingly. 'A five-day wonder... they'll forget about us soon enough.'

But Kelda was too proud to forget how their marriage must look to outsiders. A shotgun wedding. She was annoyed that she had let Angelo pressure her into marrying him before the baby was born. Instinct told her that she would not have felt so threatened by the cameras had she regained her once lithe shape instead of resembling a barrage balloon in a horribly cutesy little maternity suit.

'Do you think so?' she breathed sharply. 'You've married down, not up. Working class girl makes good. The Press like that.'

'I rather think that I'm the one who has... made good,' Angelo countered.

Her teeth clenched. What did you do with a male who set your teeth on edge with exquisite courtesy and then refused to fight? Literally she gnashed her teeth.

'I hope you like Hedley Court.'

Angelo owned an Elizabethan manor. She had never seen it. All that had struck her about her future home was that it lay almost a hundred miles from London where Angelo necessarily spent the greater part of his time. He had an apartment in town. It would be very convenient for him, wouldn't it? A wife and a child a safe hundred miles away? Well if Angelo fondly imagined that he was going to turn her into a country weekend wife, who never saw him between Monday and Friday, he was in for a surprise.

She scrutinised the fine platinum band encircling her ring finger. Put there by Angelo, sealed by a cold kiss on her brow, the sort of a salute you gave to a child. You've been behaving like one all day, a little voice said drily. Insecurity made her nervous and abrasive.

Hedley Court looked spectacular in the crisp winter sunlight. Although it was late afternoon, the temperature had stayed below freezing all day and a white frost still iced the lawns and gilded the clipped yews. As Angelo assisted her out of the car, a cold wind made her shiver. He whipped off his jacket like a cavalier and draped it round her slight shoulders.

'Don't be silly,' she hissed. 'A puff of wind isn't likely to blow me away.'

'I wish we could have gone somewhere warmer for a few weeks.' Angelo pressed her across the gravel towards the front door.

Kelda stared blindly at the beautiful frontage of the Court with its mullioned windows. A trip abroad had been quite out of the question so late in her pregnancy. Her emerald eyes were overbright. She was mentally enumerating all the frills that had been shorn from her wedding day. A gown would have looked ridiculous and she was supposed to be taking things very easy, so a lot of guests and a reception had been ruled out on that count as well. Frankly, she suspected that Angelo had been grateful for an excuse to avoid a standard society wedding adorned by an enormously pregnant bride.

Without warning, Angelo bent and swept her off her feet.

'Put me down!' she shrieked in mortification, aware that she was no lightweight, waiting to hear him grunt with surprised effort.

'This is one tradition we can fulfil,' Angelo told her, carrying her across the threshold into a giant reception hall walled with linenfold panelling.

'It's beautiful!' Kelda craned her head back for a better view of the minstrels' gallery. 'When did you buy it?'

'My great-great-grandmother married into the original Hedley family——'

Kelda reddened. She was reminded that, unlike her, Angelo had a blue-blooded family tree. Angelo didn't have to *buy* his historic house in the country. He had probably inherited it.

'I remember coming here as a child.' He set her down gently at the top of the stone stairs. 'The Court eventually came to my mother. A great-uncle of mine lived here until his death a couple of years ago.' He showed her into a beautifully furnished bedroom. 'You should lie down for a while before dinner. You can meet the staff then. They appear to have beat a tactful retreat for our arrival.'

And then he was gone. It was a very feminine bedroom. Through a door she discovered a dressing-room that led into a marvellously sybaritic bathroom. She was checking through the empty wardrobes when her cases arrived and, with them, the housekeeper, Mrs Moss, who had clearly had no intention of waiting until dinner to meet Angelo's new bride.

When Kelda eventually lay down it was almost six. She was desperately tired but all she could think about was the absence of any male clothing in the wardrobes. This was not a room which Angelo intended to share with her.

Angelo made polite pleasant conversation over dinner until she wanted to scream. It was as if a glass wall divided him from her. She needed to smash it. Fingering her glass of mineral water, she cast him a glance from beneath her long feathery lashes.

'Which one were you going to settle on?' she asked softly.

Angelo elevated an ebony brow. 'Which what?'

'Adele or Felicity or Caroline or Fiona,' Kelda specified. 'Which one made the highest score?'

Lashes as long and thicker than her own dropped low over gleaming dark eyes. 'I find that rather a loaded question.'

'But a natural one to ask. After all,' Kelda breathed sweetly, 'you've spent the past six months auditioning potential brides, and I was never on the list even to begin with. Naturally I'm curious.'

Angelo leant back in his chair, his strikingly handsome features dispassionate and infuriatingly uninformative.

The silence gathered strength and Kelda refused to be intimidated by it.

'Adele had the best pedigree——'

'Only animals have pedigree.'

Kelda smiled with scorn. 'You were clearly shopping for a pedigree, Angelo. Every one of them was upper class and rich. None of them had had previous marriages. One worked in a museum. One worked in an art gallery. And one helped Mummy with her favourite children's charity——'

'Kelda——' he murmured warningly.

'Fiona was the only one with third-level education and a *real* career. Presumably she would have been too bright and too independent for the role. On the other hand, she was the most stunning-looking,' Kelda continued in the same chatty tone, ignoring the hardening line of his expressive mouth. 'Did you make love to all of them or none of them? And how does it feel to have decided exactly what you want in a wife and then have to come down to real basics and settle on one from a council estate?'

'Without your assistance tonight, I don't think I ever would have realised how desperately insecure you are,' Angelo drawled.

She froze as though he had slapped her.

'Does sniping at me make you feel any better?' he asked drily.

He hadn't answered her questions. She threw up her head in open challenge. 'As a matter of fact, it does!'

'I think you should go to bed.' Angelo rose gracefully from his chair. 'This conversation ends here.'

She sprang upright, her cheeks flaming. 'You haven't answered me!'

'And I'm not likely to...in the mood that you are in now.'

He walked out of the dining-room. She followed him to the door. 'We've only been married for eight hours and I'm bored stiff!' she flung.

He swung back, cast her a glittering, hard smile. 'I would hate to be the only one suffering.'

That hurt. That hurt much more than she could have believed. She cried herself to sleep. What had she wanted? What had she expected? Reassurance, tenderness, affection. Only a man in love would give her those responses. And Angelo didn't love her. It was their wedding-night, and because sex was out of the question he didn't bother coming near her at all. Eight hours and already she was wondering if she had made the greatest mistake of her life.

He apologised over breakfast. Very smoothly. In fact, he had a positive spring in his step and he smiled several times over nothing in particular. He told her that he would be back for dinner, reminded her yet again that he could be reached at all times by his mobile phone, and strode out to the helicopter that had arrived to pick him up.

He was less stiff over dinner that evening. For some reason, he was in an utterly charming mood. He suggested outrageous names for the baby, informed her that he was taking time off to accompany her to all her checkups and dragged her upstairs to view the room he had decided would best suit as a nursery. They argued amicably about that. She went to bed that night, frantically wondering what had brought about his altered mood and hoping that it would last.

It did. Over the next three weeks, Angelo took part in every aspect of preparing for a new baby. He looked at the wallpaper books, wandered through nursery furniture displays and was quite touchingly astounded at the tiny size of newborn clothing.

Four days after that, Kelda went into labour. She did not initially appreciate that the increasing ache in her back was anything to worry about. By the time that she did, it was too late to give Angelo sufficient warning to get back from Glasgow, where he was involved with an international conference.

She gave birth at the local cottage hospital and not the fancy clinic Angelo had expected her to use. Her labour only lasted two hours and she was delighted, only slightly miffed when she heard the middle-aged midwife say something about 'good childbearing hips'! Angelo arrived long after the excitement was over.

'Don't you think you could have given me more warning?' he drawled from the threshold of her room.

'I didn't get much warning either.' She sat up, flushed and tired but consumed with pride. 'Look at her,' she demanded.

Angelo was very pale. He tiptoed over to the side of the cot and peered in. Their daughter chose that moment to squall. 'Terrific lungs,' he murmured, searching the tiny infuriated face. 'My hair, your nose...'

Her heart sunk. Was he searching for Rossetti genes? Was there still a shadow of doubt? Almost defensively, Kelda reached for her baby. 'She's got your eyes.'

'I suppose you didn't call me in time because you didn't really want me here,' Angelo asserted without a flicker of expression.

'There wasn't time!'

But she could see that he didn't believe her. And, if she was honest, she wouldn't have wanted him in the delivery-room. In the current state of their relationship, she would have shrunk from sharing something that intimate.

Was he disappointed that she wasn't a boy? He sank down on the edge of the bed and reached for a tiny hand, awkwardly traced a little froglike leg. He studied their child intently and wiped quite unselfconsciously at his dampened eyes. 'May I hold her?'

When he replaced her in the cot, he stared back at Kelda, fierce emotion unhidden in his golden gaze. 'No matter what happens between us in the future... thank you for her.'

Kelda had to bow her head to hide her tears. She had somehow expected him to put his arms around her, maybe even kiss her, but he didn't touch her at all. The only female in the room that Angelo couldn't keep his hands off weighed less than seven pounds, and if *she* cried she got instant attention. Kelda had never experienced a more savage sense of rejection.

CHAPTER TEN

'ALICE, my darling, you have it made!' Gina exclaimed, taking in the full glory of the nursery suite with astonished eyes. 'Is there anything you haven't bought this child yet, Kelda? A solid gold toothbrush in waiting for the first tooth?'

'Ask Angelo,' Kelda suggested rather tightly, returning her daughter to her four-poster cot. 'The world's biggest shopper at Hamley's.'

'And you're complaining? Some men don't want anything to do with their kids——'

'Nobody will ever angle that accusation at Angelo.'

'Do I sense a sour note in paradise?'

Kelda straightened with a fixed smile. 'No. Maybe I'm just a little tired.'

Gina giggled. 'Burning the candle at *both* ends?' she teased. 'New baby and a new marriage hardly out of the honeymoon phase. No wonder you've got shadows!'

Kelda forced a laugh. She wasn't tempted to weep on a friendly shoulder. The truth was so hideously humiliating. Alice was seven weeks old and their marriage hadn't even been consummated. Angelo had his bedroom; she had hers. No floorboards creaked in the middle of the night. Angelo clearly had his sights set on an annulment, rather than a divorce.

'If I didn't have Russ, I'd be green with envy!' Gina sighed helplessly. 'He's gorgeous, super-rich and crazy about Alice.'

Alice was all they shared. Alice was all they talked about in any depth. If Kelda hadn't adored her daughter with equal intensity, she would have been enduring agonies of jealousy. As it was, she felt disturbingly *used*. Angelo had wanted his child to carry his name. Angelo

166

had wanted to ensure that he had maximum rights over that same child and those rights were only granted by the institution of marriage.

Angelo had persuaded her into marriage for very good reasons. But they all related to Alice. Kelda might have found it possible to forgive him for that to some extent had he not pretended that he wanted *her* equally. She felt sick inside when she recalled how much that belief had encouraged her to hope that they could have a real marriage. She had been so mortifyingly certain that Angelo found her ragingly desirable...until she married him. Now, she knew different.

And it was time she did something about it, she acknowledged unhappily. Time she took charge of her own future again. She had tried marriage to Angelo and she didn't like it. That was all she had ever promised to do. She did not need Angelo to survive. Ella Donaldson had called last month and had intimated that Kelda could virtually dictate terms for a new contract should she wish to enter the modelling world again.

Angelo was very entertaining over dinner. Russ and Gina were most impressed. Kelda's temper rose steadily throughout the meal. When she dined with Angelo alone, he was polite and distant. As soon as her friends had departed, Angelo strode off to the library which he used as an office. Five minutes later, Kelda decided to invade his privacy.

Angelo was not deep in work as she had expected. He was standing by the fireplace with a large whiskey in his hand, his darkly handsome features shadowed and taut.

'We need to talk,' Kelda said tightly, suppressing the sizzling leap of awareness which always consumed her near Angelo. In the past two months she had learnt to be ashamed of that sexual *frisson*.

He offered her a drink which she declined.

Kelda breathed in deeply. Pride demanded that she make the first move to the break. 'I think we should go for an annulment as soon as possible.'

'I beg your pardon?' Angelo said very quietly, narrowed dark eyes nailed to her with perceptible force.

Kelda wandered over to the window, her body tensing in response to the thickening atmosphere. 'Look, this isn't working for either of us,' she pointed out in a driven rush. 'I'll move out——'

'You take Alice from this house over my dead body,' Angelo spelt out dangerously softly.

'You can see as much of her as you like. I'll be going back to work anyway,' Kelda told him.

'Really?'

She flushed. 'Why the hell shouldn't I if I want to?'

'Country life too quiet for you?'

She was tempted to tell him that it was the nights. 'We don't have a real marriage,' she muttered jerkily.

'I can change that any time you care to ask.'

Kelda flinched from his sarcasm. 'I want an annulment and you can't stop me from getting one!' she stated, and walked hurriedly back out of the room and upstairs.

There it was done. He hadn't said much. Then Angelo liked to call his own shots. She had stolen his thunder. Doubtless he had planned for this farce to continue for a few more months. Dear lord, she conceded painfully, she had been so appallingly blind and trusting and stupid... and with Angelo of all people! Angelo was notorious for his calculating, brilliant moves on the international money market.

When he had first mentioned marriage, he had been honest. He had suggested a fake marriage to keep the family happy and give their child his name. A fake marriage and a convincing breakdown followed by separation and divorce. And how had she reacted? She had made it furiously clear that she would not even consider such a hypocritical deception. So Angelo had reinvented his case for marriage in terms calculated to win her acceptance.

She had fallen like a ton of bricks for that line because she loved him, and up until Alice's birth Angelo had played along. But from that same day, he had changed. Damp-eyed, Kelda slid into the cool embrace of her bed. Her thoughts were in frantic turmoil. Had Angelo actually believed that eventually she would get bored with motherhood and walk away, leaving Alice behind with him? Was that his ultimate goal?

He would acquire Alice, go for an annulment and then remarry someone more suitable. It was Machiavellian...it was Angelo. Since Alice's birth, he had been trying to freeze her out. All his emotional warmth was fully concentrated on their daughter. He had left Kelda out in the cold. As the door opened, she lifted her head and her emerald eyes opened to their fullest extent.

'Whatever we end up with, it won't be an annulment,' Angelo drawled silkily, glittering dark eyes raking her startled face.

He was wearing a black silk robe and nothing else. In one hand he had an uncorked bottle of champagne, two glasses in the other. Blinking bemusedly, Kelda simply stared as he deftly filled the glasses. He had settled one into her hand before she found her tongue again.

'What do you think you're doing in here?'

Angelo cast off the robe without a shade of inhibition. For a split-second her gaze was involuntarily welded to the lean, dark magnificence of his powerful physique. Hot colour drenched her complexion as he pushed back the sheet and slid gracefully into bed beside her.

'Angelo...'

He brushed his glass against hers. 'Say goodbye to months of sexual abstinence,' he murmured. 'If this is what you want, I am more than willing to oblige.'

'What *I* want?' She gave a sudden gasp of shock as he quite deliberately angled his glass over one pouting breast almost completely bared by the slipping sheet and let champagne drip over her heated flesh. 'A-Angelo!'

Her own glass dropped from her nerveless fingers and fell soundlessly on the floor.

'I would hate to think your boredom might extend to what I intend to do to you in bed,' Angelo breathed, hauling the sheet down with a determined hand and tipping her roughly back against the pillows.

'Stop it! I don't want this!' she cried, so shocked she had trouble framing the words.

'You've been gasping for it for weeks. You think I don't know that? Do you fondly imagine that I can't tell when a woman wants me?'

'You swine!' she launched, beside herself with rage and disbelief.

He bent his dark head and found the lush dampness of her nipple and her whole body jerked in electrified excitement. Her hands squeezed into fists as she fought the raw overload on her senses. It had been so long and she wanted him so badly. She could feel herself quaking on the edge of that wildness he had roused in her before. It was terrifyingly intense.

He followed the sweet trail of the champagne down over her quivering stomach and she made a sudden grab at his hair. 'No!'

But his hands were on her thighs and he had already discovered just how weak she really was. She was tender and damp.

'Evidently I wasn't the only one seething with silent lust over dinner,' Angelo murmured huskily, letting the tip of his tongue track the clenched muscles on her inner thigh until she trembled and shook and completely forgot that she was supposed to be fighting him off.

She shut her eyes, her heartbeat like a hammer pounding in her eardrums, and nothing existed but Angelo and what he was doing to her. She had never imagined...had never dreamt that she would let *anyone*...but she couldn't have stopped him, couldn't possibly have regained control of her shudderingly responsive body. He had devastated her with a depth of intimacy far beyond her limited experience and she was utterly overpowered by the incredible waves of pleasure.

She heard her own voice rising, heard herself moan his name over and over again and then her back arched and her teeth clenched and her wild cry of release was literally torn from her as he sent her plunging into a climax that blocked the whole world out for timeless minutes.

'Maybe you'll deign to smile at me over dinner tomorrow night,' Angelo said roughly, sliding up over her and taking her mouth with explosive passion.

He ground his hips into her pelvis, letting her know just how aroused he was while his tongue possessed her mouth in a raw imitation of a far more basic sexual union. Hard hands tugged her thighs apart and he lifted his head, golden eyes stabbing into glazed green as he thrust slowly into the quivering depths of her body.

He thrust deeper; she melted. He moved; she moaned.

'Bored?' Angelo demanded thickly.

The sole response he received was a panted attempt to breathe at the peak of the most unimaginable pleasure.

'Tell me you want me.' He rolled over, carrying her with him, and let his mouth enclose the engorged tip of one sensitive breast.

'All the time...oh, God, don't stop...!' she almost sobbed as he mercilessly stilled.

'No divorce.' A lean hand wound with painful thoroughness into the cascading tangle of her red hair.

'Angelo...' she pleaded.

'No divorce.'

'No divorce.' She would have done anything, said anything, sold herself into white slavery for the next half-century just for him to continue. Tuscany all those months ago could not have prepared her for the savage seduction of what he was now making her feel.

He made love to her with smouldering sensuality and wild passion. He drove her over the edge of ecstasy more than once, and when he finally took his own pleasure she buried her tear-stained face into the sweat-slicked muscularity of one powerful shoulder and clung, still shivering with tiny after-shocks.

'I hate to tell you this, but your mother was right,' Angelo murmured in a black velvet purr as she abstractedly pressed tiny kisses against whatever part of him was within reach as he shifted languorously against her. 'You can't keep your hands off me. Think of how humiliated you would feel as an ex-wife, still falling into my bed at every opportunity...'

Kelda froze, dragged from her sensual languor by sheer shock.

She collided with incandescent golden eyes as fierce as knives. 'And don't think I wouldn't take advantage,' Angelo drawled softly, savagely. 'I *would*. I'd be the wolf at your door, and every time I got you flat on your back I'd make you pay a hundred times over for the divorce. Does that prospect appeal to you?'

Shattered, she stared up at him, her blood chilling in her veins, pallor driving away her natural colour.

'I think we understand each other perfectly, *cara*.' Angelo scored a mocking forefinger along the reddened fullness of her lower lip. 'And since regular sex appears to be the key to that locked-tight, unforgiving little heart of yours, I don't think you'll have any complaints in the future.'

'Get out of here!' she launched, relocating her ready tongue.

Angelo reached out, switched off the lamp and reached for her with arms that brooked no argument. 'Any bed you occupy will also be occupied by me from now on.'

'I won't stand——'

'You'd be surprised what I can make you stand,' he whispered mockingly.

She was feeding Alice at six in the morning when he strolled into the nursery.

She felt ridiculously shy of him. He crouched down in front of her and ran a caressing thumb along the downy line of Alice's cheek. Her lustrous dark eyes swivelled and she gave an angry squawk round the bottle. Their daughter did not like to be disturbed when she was feeding.

Kelda was in turmoil. Yesterday she had been convinced that a separation was the only answer. Yesterday, she had believed that Angelo no longer wanted her. And then last night... well, last night had completely wiped out her every assumption. Angelo had destroyed any prospect of either of them seeking an annulment and had then gone on to ruthlessly delineate what would happen if she sought a divorce.

He had talked as though all she needed from him was sex. She reddened, wondered dismally if he found her abandonment and eagerness abnormal. He touched her and, frankly, everything else went out of the window. She felt enslaved by what he could make her feel both physically and emotionally. When he made love to her, it made her feel so *close* to him. She needed that closeness to survive.

'I'm going to Geneva. I'll be away until tomorrow evening,' he divulged. 'Start looking for a good nanny. If Alice has you all day, I expect to have you all night.'

She jerked as he sent a possessive hand skimming over a slender thigh, exposed by her carelessly parted robe.

'And at dawn,' Angelo added huskily.

'I thought you didn't think a nanny was——'

'I've changed my mind.'

It was the following morning that the sound of constantly ringing phones woke Kelda up from a sound sleep. She always went back to bed for a couple of hours after feeding Alice. After a quick shower, she went down for breakfast, dressed in a figure-hugging apple-green dress that made her feel like a million dollars. Green was also Angelo's favourite colour... dear lord, was she turning into a doormat?

The newspaper she normally read over breakfast was missing from the pile. As Mrs Moss came in with her coffee, she asked for it, and the instant she saw the older woman's strained face she knew that something was badly wrong.

'You want that one, Mrs Rossetti?' the older woman prompted unnecessarily.

'Yes.' Kelda frowned. 'Is something up, Mrs Moss?'

The housekeeper cleared her throat. 'Your mother phoned to say she was coming over straight away.'

A cold hand clutched at Kelda's heart. 'Why were the phones ringing?'

'Newspaper reporters, Mrs Rossetti . . . would you like me to disconnect them?'

'No . . .' Slowly Kelda stood up, her face as white as a sheet. Why was her mother coming over? Why hadn't her mother asked to speak directly to her? Her stomach churned with sick horror. Her mind rushed to burning visions of plane crashes and explosions and car accidents and Angelo starred in every disaster. 'Angelo . . .' she whispered. 'Has something happened to Angelo?'

'Good heavens, no!' Mrs Moss hurried to reassure her. 'It's just that dreadful newspaper, that's all!'

'Newspaper . . . what newspaper?' The one missing from the pile, she gasped, absolutely sick and weak-kneed with relief that whatever was wrong did not involve injury of any kind to Angelo. 'Could I see it, please?'

Something upsetting—hardly a new experience, she thought, watching the housekeeper's reluctant reappearance with the item. 'Thanks,' she said.

Mrs Moss looked even more tense. 'Your mother didn't want you to see it until she arrived . . .'

The front page was practically all headline. 'The Banker and the Bank-robber's daughter.' What a mouthful, she thought, until she focused incredulously on the photo beneath. It was a picture of Angelo and her on their wedding-day.

She began reading, her heart hammering sickly behind her breastbone. It hurt to breathe. She had to read every melodramatic sentence at least twice over to understand it. Shock was starting to take over. But it was complete and utter rubbish and she would sue, she told herself. Even Angelo would back her on that! How dared these vultures print such monstrous lies about her father! Her father had never been in prison in his life! Clearly they had got him mixed up with somebody else. Outrage began to take over from shock.

'K-Kelda?' She lifted her head from her taut stance by the table.

Her mother stood several feet away, her face a mask of distress. 'You've seen it?' She hesitated, her hands tightly clasped together. 'I am so sorry.'

'*Sorry*?' Kelda echoed in disbelief. 'What have you got to be sorry about? We'll sue! They're the ones who'll be sorry!'

'But it's true,' Daisy practically whispered. 'Every word of it is true.'

Kelda stared back at her mother, willing her to take that unbelievable statement back. 'Dad worked abroad on an oil-field,' she said drily.

Daisy flinched and tearfully shook her head. 'Tomaso was right. I should have told you the truth years ago. I should never have lied. Steve was in and out of prison practically from when you were born. He stole cars. He burgled houses. Of c-course,' she stammered painfully, 'he wasn't very good at it. He always got caught.'

Kelda couldn't stay upright any longer. It was like a nightmare. Her whole childhood was suddenly caving in beneath her feet. She collapsed down in a chair, trembling like a leaf and sick to her stomach.

'When you were a baby, I used to take you to visit him,' her mother told her. 'That was when I still thought he would go straight and I tried to be loyal and supportive. I was crazy about him at the beginning. He was so much fun, so handsome, so exciting. But every time he let us down again, a little bit of the love died——'

'Oh, God, no...' Kelda mumbled, totally devastated.

'You see, he didn't really mind prison with his mates.
The sentences were always short. I used to plead with
him. He used to make all these promises...but he always
broke them. We moved all around the country. One new
start after another. I was so ashamed. And then, when
you were seven, Steve took part in a bank robbery,' Daisy
told her shakily. 'A security guard was hurt. That was
serious crime. He was put away for years...'

'But the letters!' Kelda suddenly shouted at her mother
in a tempest of anger and humiliation. She refused to
believe that what she was hearing could possibly be true.

'I didn't want you to know. You loved him so much.'
Her mother shot her a pleading look. 'He loved telling
you those stories. He had a terrific imagination. Don't
you understand, Kelda?' Daisy sobbed. 'Steve was only
nineteen when you were born and he never really grew
up. He wanted so badly to keep on being your hero and
that was the only way he could...'

Kelda covered her contorted face with both hands.

'I might as well tell you all of it,' her mother muttered
grudgingly. 'I met Tomaso three years before your father
died!'

Kelda bent her head and looked away in an agony of
pain and rejection.

'For both of us, it was love at first sight. Tomaso
wanted me to divorce Steve but I couldn't do that, not
when he was locked away with nothing but us on the
outside to live for. So I kept on visiting, kept on pretending that everything was all right,' Daisy shared
wretchedly. 'But I couldn't stop seeing Tomaso. I tried
to several times——'

'*You* were his mistress,' Kelda framed sickly, thinking
of the time she had been told about the blonde Tomaso
had been taking away to discreet country pubs for years.
That blonde had been Daisy.

'No! I never ever took a penny of financial help from
Tomaso!' Daisy protested vehemently. 'I *loved* him,
Kelda, the way I think you love Angelo. And he was

prepared to wait for me to be free, no matter how long it took, and he would have waited. Your father's heart attack was a total shock. He was a very young man when he died——'

'Conveniently,' Kelda could not resist saying, and then covered her face again, suddenly ashamed. 'I'm sorry, I didn't mean that. You must have had so much unhappiness with Dad——'

'My marriage to Tomaso broke up the first time because of guilt,' Daisy whispered unsteadily. 'I couldn't live with my conscience. I couldn't allow myself to be happy because I had been disloyal to your father and in the end I simply couldn't cope. It was only when I was away from Tomaso that I was able to sort my feelings out. Your father made his choices, Kelda. I wasn't responsible for them. He put himself in prison. He didn't much care what that did to us as a family. He was too irresponsible to think of anybody but himself...'

Silence greeted that final speech. Kelda was rocking soundlessly back and forth on her chair, fathoms deep in shock as her mind skipped agilely over her childhood and saw all the inconsistencies she had innocently accepted. She was shattered.

'Tim has known for a couple of years.'

Kelda choked back angry words of desperate hurt. She should have been told the truth a long, long time ago.

'I wish Angelo had known!' Her mother suddenly burst into tears.

Kelda was dragged from her stupor with a vengeance.

'How do you think Angelo will react to this?' Daisy sobbed. 'Worse, finding out about it in a newspaper!'

Tomaso came in, looking grim and strained. He comforted her mother while Kelda simply stood there in the grip of a horror that put everything she had previously experienced into the nursery stakes. Yes, how *would* Angelo react to the humiliation of the discovery that he was married to the daughter of a criminal? A criminal who had robbed a bank, of all things!

'I don't blame you, Mum.' Abruptly unfreezing, Kelda rushed to put her arms round her sobbing parent. 'You did the best you could.'

'But if this damages your marriage, I'll never forgive myself!'

'Angelo is on his way back from Geneva,' Tomaso sighed. 'We'll stay, deal with this as a family should.'

'No...' Kelda was appalled by the suggestion. She didn't want an inhibiting audience when Angelo came home. That wouldn't be fair to him.

It took persuasion but finally Tomaso and Daisy left. It would be hours before Angelo got back. Kelda darted upstairs and dug out the worn and faded stationery box in which she kept her father's letters. Anguish had returned, only now it was strengthened by fear.

What chance did their marriage have now? Angelo *had* unwittingly married the bank-robber's daughter. A lot of people were going to find that hilariously funny. And what about the rumour that he was soon to be offered the position of chief executive in the Rossetti Industrial Bank? Wasn't there a possibility that that too could be affected by his unfortunate marriage?

With scorching tears in her eyes, Kelda went in search of her suitcases. An hour later, she had packed. She was totally choked up by then. Her swollen eyes fell on the box of her father's letters and with sudden explosive bitterness, she sped downstairs to ask Mrs Moss for matches. Crouching down in front of the fireplace in her bedroom, she shook out the first letter, tears streaming down her face. The paper was worn thin by repeated readings, the ink faded.

She struck the first match and a split-second later there was a sudden step behind her and a hand snatched the match from her before she could ignite the letters piled in the grate. Still on her knees, she spun. 'What the heck do you...Angelo!' she gasped. 'But...but you're not due back until——'

'I cancelled my meetings and flew back immediately.'

Wordlessly she stared up at him. He reached down and raised her up but she wouldn't meet his eyes. She was drowning in angry humiliation. He already knew. Someone had told him. Why else would he arrive back early?

'Why were you about to burn your father's letters?'

'That's a very s-stupid question,' Kelda stammered.

'Once they're gone, they're gone, and those letters are all that you have of him,' Angelo pointed out almost gently.

The confrontation was not going in any expected direction. Her brow furrowed. 'Those letters are full of nothing but lies!'

'Does that really matter so much?' Angelo smoothed a straying curl from her damp temples. 'Your father loved you. He must have spent hours writing them and they made you happy when you were a child. Those letters made you feel secure and loved——'

'But they were *lies*!' Unable to comprehend why he was behaving this way, Kelda almost screamed at him and attempted to pull free.

'And don't you think your mother had something to do with that? Whose idea do you think it was that he should pretend to be working abroad rather than admit the truth?'

Kelda's breath escaped shakily.

'It was probably your mother's, and her motives were very much based on protecting you. She wanted you to have a father you could admire, a father you could talk about freely with your friends... it was an utterly insane charade but it kept you happy. You were safe in Liverpool. But you would have found out the truth if he had lived,' Angelo murmured intently, holding her fast by her shoulders. 'Sooner or later, you might have discovered that there is *no* oil in Jordan...'

'No oil?' she echoed dazedly.

'No oil. He couldn't have been working on an oil-field there.'

She frowned up at him. 'In Italy,' she whispered. 'You *knew*! But you said nothing...'

Lustrous dark eyes arrowed over her distressed face. 'I was curious to find out exactly how much you did know. You see, *cara*...I've known for almost ten years——'

'But you couldn't have——' she broke in, her eyes clinging to his.

'When my father married Daisy, I already knew they had been having a very discreet affair. The sudden marriage shook me as much as you,' he confided wryly. 'I ran a security check on your mother and the report was very thorough. I'm afraid to say that I didn't interpret the facts with much generosity. A late husband, who had been a regular prison inmate, two children stashed conveniently in another city. Haven't you ever wondered why I misjudged your mother so badly then?'

Kelda was shaken. Angelo had always known. Angelo had known from the beginning.

'I was only twenty-two and rather arrogant. I couldn't understand why my father had married her...'

She was remembering Angelo's cold antagonism towards her mother and suddenly she could understand why he had been so prejudiced from the outset.

'I had to become a little more mature before I could accept that the sinner was not your mother,' Angelo imparted quietly. 'And that, when you love somebody, you accept *everything* about that person, not just the facets that you like.'

'You knew...' She was still fumbling with that discovery. 'And yet you never threw it at me...not even when I accused your father of having a mistress and you probably knew then that the other woman was in fact my own mother——'

'Yes,' he sighed.

Why was he being kind and understanding? Kelda trembled, her emotions still raw and bleeding from her traumatic morning. 'Well, why didn't you throw it in my face?'

'When you were a child, I wouldn't have hurt you, and when you were almost an adult I still wouldn't have hurt you.' Angelo brushed a caressing hand gently over her wobbling lower lip. 'And when you became an adult I found that I *couldn't* hurt you.'

'But why?' she whispered.

He expelled his breath and abruptly let his hands drop from her. 'Because when you were sixteen I fell in love with you . . . and somehow I never quite managed to fall out of love again,' he said harshly.

The confession froze her in her tracks. He was standing with his back to her by the window, the muscles in his broad shoulders clearly clenched with tension beneath the well-cut jacket.

'Evidently I'm a one-woman man.' Fierce satire edged the statement. 'Six years ago I wanted to marry you because I loved you. Of course, you were far too young and you were not in love with me——'

Distantly she recalled him telling her in Tuscany how bitterly he had resented being forced into playing a father figure when Tomaso opted out. And finally she understood why. She also understood why he had gone over the edge that night when he'd found her in the library with that boy.

'I spent the past six years haunted by you. I framed that *Vogue* cover. It hangs in the bedroom of my London apartment.'

'Angelo . . .' she muttered softly, shock receding, delight and the most humbling sense of gratitude taking her over.

'*Dio* . . . do you think I want your pity?' he slashed back at her, swinging round. 'All those years reading about your other men! At times, I hated you more than I loved you. I brought you to Tuscany because I believed that you were really only a fantasy. If I actually made

love to you, I believed, the fantasy would die. Only it
didn't. It simply got me in deeper!'

'I thought you were a sexual infatuation,' Kelda told
him dry-mouthed.

'I can live with that,' Angelo shot at her grimly. 'I
can live with that better than losing you.'

'You're not going to lose me.' She smiled almost shyly
at him.

'Then perhaps you can tell me why you have packed?'
he demanded not quite steadily, pallor visible beneath
his dark skin.

'I was being really stupid...I thought you'd be so
angry and humiliated about the story in the paper——'

'All I had time to worry about was what that story
was doing to you. Why should I be angry? It was your
feelings I was most concerned about.'

The truth of that had been so plain from the moment
he'd stopped her impulsively burning her father's letters
that her throat closed over with tears. All the tenderness
and caring she had ever sought had been there for her
instantly. 'If you love me, why have you been so aloof
since Alice was born?' she asked helplessly.

'I wanted to be with you when she was born. It was
so obvious that that would not have been your choice...I
felt rejected,' he breathed tautly. 'I had tried so hard
before that to make you relax with me and I thought I
was getting somewhere...then I realised I wasn't.
Treating you like a sort of sister had been such a
strain——'

'A strain for me too. I thought you found my
shape...revolting,' she confided in a rush. 'You never
touched me.'

'I didn't think you would allow me to. I was trying to
build a bond of trust between us. I had made such a
mess of our relationship in Tuscany. I went overboard
that night at Daisy's cottage,' he relived unsteadily,
beautiful golden eyes clinging to her intent face. 'I

couldn't trust myself near you. I was scared I would make an even bigger fool of myself.'

'You didn't make a fool of yourself that night. If only I hadn't lied, if only we had talked ... *really* talked,' she said with bitter regret.

'I wanted so badly to hear that your baby was mine,' Angelo confessed roughly. 'Couldn't you see that?'

Kelda had paled. 'Even though you thought I had slept with Russ?'

'Yes,' he admitted ruefully.

'All I could think about was Fiona,' she admitted. 'My pride was hurt. I was bitter and hurt and jealous and I really did believe that the last thing you wanted to hear was that the baby was yours.'

'You were wrong. And when I realised that you had lied, I think that was the worst rejection of all. I thought you had to really hate me to have lied. You didn't even consider telling me the truth or approaching me for help all those months that you were pregnant,' he pointed out. 'That stood between us from the hour I married you...that even pregnant and alone you wanted nothing to do with me.'

The pain that conviction had given him was in his dark eyes.

Kelda shook her head. 'That never even occurred to me. All I could think about was Adele and all the other women——'

'I haven't slept with anyone but you since Italy.' Angelo absorbed her incredulity and a slanting smile tilted his handsome mouth. 'Not even come near it. I couldn't have used another woman just for sexual release when the only woman I really wanted was you.'

'Not even Fiona?'

Angelo laughed heartily. 'She dumped me the day after the wedding. She said she wouldn't be used to make another woman jealous but that if I ever got over you she might give me a second chance.' He hesitated. 'Did you use the food in the hampers?'

'Hampers?' Kelda repeated, her brow creasing. 'From Harrods? *You sent them*?'

'Didn't you even suspect?'

'I thought your father was behind them!' Kelda groaned. 'I never would have dreamt that they were from you... not after the way we parted at the cottage.'

'You were so thin.' One of his hands clenched and he shrugged jerkily. 'I wanted to be sure you ate properly...'

She was unbearably touched that he had been concerned about her even when he'd believed that her child was not his. Her whole face glowed. 'I love you, Angelo.' It was extraordinary how much courage it took to say it.

His brilliant eyes narrowed, his hard, dark features tightening, and then suddenly he reached for her, his lean hands bruising. 'You don't need to say that!'

'I fell in love in Tuscany. Maybe it was the emeralds that did it,' she teased, pressing her lips against his throat, breathing in the gloriously familiar scent of him with sensual pleasure. 'Or being flung in jail. Or maybe it had been brewing for six years and it was just waiting for an opportunity to blaze. But the fact is, Angelo, I am absolutely crazy about you too!'

'I thought the only thing you wanted was my body——'

'I hope it's included in the package.' She ran a flagrantly possessive hand over the breadth of his chest. 'And by the way,' she added, in a uniquely generous mood, letting her whole body rest against him, 'I haven't had any other lovers...'

He tensed, collided with her amused gaze and suddenly crushed her mouth hotly beneath his. It was a couple of hours before a sensible word was spoken again. Curved round Angelo's sprawling length, Kelda suddenly jerked and gasped, 'Alice! I forgot about her!'

'Inga will be with her.' Angelo trapped her with a powerful arm before she could move.

'Inga?'

'I brought her back from Geneva. I dined with friends last night. Inga had been with their children for several years. They don't need her any more and she was working out her last week, so after I'd heard a glowing testimonial and talked to her, I engaged her on the spot and brought her home with me.'

'Inga. Swedish?'

'Her English is excellent.'

'Danny Philips ran off with his children's nanny,' Kelda couldn't help remarking. 'I suppose she's blonde.'

'Jealous little cat,' Angelo breathed in her ear. 'She's fifty and built like a tank.'

'Oh.' Kelda relaxed.

'I'm sorry about your father,' he murmured. 'But he wasn't the hardened criminal the newspaper made out. He was never involved in any form of violence——'

'But the bank robbery——'

'He was the driver and he was unarmed. He put a stocking mask over his face, double parked in the wrong street just round the corner of a police station and blew the whole show for his partners in crime. A bit inept, your father.'

Kelda found that she was trying not to laugh. It still hurt, but reality was better than a fairy story. If Angelo could live with it, she could still hold her head high. 'I love you,' she told him fiercely, staring down at him.

'Enough to stay forever and ever?' Angelo enquired silkily, running a lean hand possessively over one slanted cheekbone.

'Are you likely to be a good investment?'

'Highly profitable,' he promised, sensually capturing her parted lips with his. 'As well as loyal, loving and constantly in a state of arousal round you,' he virtually completed on a groan.

'And the next time I have a baby you'll——'

'Be there, share everything.'

'You learn fast.' Kelda slid a provocative hand over his flat hard stomach and smiled at his instantaneous response.

'Move fast too.' With a husky laugh, he pinned her flat. 'How does the idea of six weeks in Tuscany appeal to you?'

'The peach and cherry orchard.' She sighed luxuriously.

'*Si* . . .' And for a long time the rest of the world was forgotten as they lost themselves and yet found each other in loving.

Take 4 bestselling love stories FREE
Plus get a FREE surprise gift!

Special Limited-time Offer

Mail to Harlequin Reader Service®

3010 Walden Avenue
P.O. Box 1867
Buffalo, N.Y. 14269-1867

YES! Please send me 4 free Harlequin Presents® novels and my free surprise gift. Then send me 6 brand-new novels every month, which I will receive months before they appear in bookstores. Bill me at the low price of $2.44 each plus 25¢ delivery and applicable sales tax, if any*. That's the complete price and—compared to the cover prices of $2.99 each—quite a bargain! I understand that accepting the books and gift places me under no obligation ever to buy any books. I can always return a shipment and cancel at any time. Even if I never buy another book from Harlequin, the 4 free books and the surprise gift are mine to keep forever.

106 BPA ANRH

Name	(PLEASE PRINT)
Address	Apt. No.
City	State	Zip

This offer is limited to one order per household and not valid to present Harlequin Presents® subscribers. *Terms and prices are subject to change without notice. Sales tax applicable in N.Y.

UPRES-94R   ©1990 Harlequin Enterprises Limited

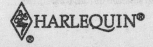

HARLEQUIN®

Don't miss these Harlequin favorites by some of our most distinguished authors!
And now, you can receive a discount by ordering two or more titles!

HT#25577	WILD LIKE THE WIND by Janice Kaiser	$2.99	☐
HT#25589	THE RETURN OF CAINE O'HALLORAN by JoAnn Ross	$2.99	☐
HP#11626	THE SEDUCTION STAKES by Lindsay Armstrong	$2.99	☐
HP#11647	GIVE A MAN A BAD NAME by Roberta Leigh	$2.99	☐
HR#03293	THE MAN WHO CAME FOR CHRISTMAS by Bethany Campbell	$2.89	☐
HR#03308	RELATIVE VALUES by Jessica Steele	$2.89	☐
SR#70589	CANDY KISSES by Muriel Jensen	$3.50	☐
SR#70598	WEDDING INVITATION by Marisa Carroll	$3.50 U.S. $3.99 CAN.	☐
HI#22230	CACHE POOR by Margaret St. George	$2.99	☐
HAR#16515	NO ROOM AT THE INN by Linda Randall Wisdom	$3.50	☐
HAR#16520	THE ADVENTURESS by M.J. Rodgers	$3.50	☐
HS#28795	PIECES OF SKY by Marianne Willman	$3.99	☐
HS#28824	A WARRIOR'S WAY by Margaret Moore	$3.99 U.S. $4.50 CAN.	☐

(limited quantities available on certain titles)

	AMOUNT	$
DEDUCT:	10% DISCOUNT FOR 2+ BOOKS	$
ADD:	POSTAGE & HANDLING	$
	($1.00 for one book, 50¢ for each additional)	
	APPLICABLE TAXES*	$_____
	TOTAL PAYABLE	$_____
	(check or money order—please do not send cash)	

To order, complete this form and send it, along with a check or money order for the total above, payable to Harlequin Books, to: **In the U.S.:** 3010 Walden Avenue, P.O. Box 9047, Buffalo, NY 14269-9047; **In Canada:** P.O. Box 613, Fort Erie, Ontario, L2A 5X3.

Name: _____

Address: _____ City: _____

State/Prov.: _____ Zip/Postal Code: _____

*New York residents remit applicable sales taxes.
Canadian residents remit applicable GST and provincial taxes.

HBACK-JM2